Lions & Liars

Kate Beasley

illustrations by Dan Santat

SQUARE FISH

FARRAR STRAUS GIROUX · NEW YORK

For Cassie

SQUARE
FISH

An imprint of Macmillan Publishing Group, LLC
175 Fifth Avenue, New York, NY 10010
mackids.com

Square Fish and the Square Fish logo are trademarks of Macmillan and
are used by Farrar Straus Giroux under license from Macmillan.

Our books may be purchased in bulk for promotional, educational,
or business use. Please contact your local bookseller or the
Macmillan Corporate and Premium Sales Department at (800) 221-7945
ext. 5442 or by email at MacmillanSpecialMarkets@macmillan.com.

Library of Congress Cataloging-in-Publication Data

Names: Beasley, Kate, author. | Santat, Dan, illustrator.
Title: Lions & liars / by Kate Beasley ; illustrated by Dan Santat.
Other titles: Lions and liars
Description: New York : Farrar Straus Giroux, 2018. | Summary:
   Fifth-grader Frederick is sent to a disciplinary camp, where
   he and his terrifying troop mates have just started forging a friendship
   when they learn a Category 5 hurricane is headed their way.
Identifiers: LCCN 2017042319 | ISBN 978-1-250-30851-1 (paperback) |
   ISBN 978-0-374-30265-8 (ebook)
Subjects: | CYAC: Camps—Fiction. | Behavior—Fiction. | Friendship—
Fiction. | Hurricanes—Fiction. | Survival—Fiction.
Classification: LCC PZ7.1.B433 Lio 2018 | DDC [Fic]—dc23
LC record available at https://lccn.loc.gov/2017042319

Originally published in the United States by Farrar Straus Giroux
First Square Fish edition, 2019
Book designed by Elizabeth H. Clark
Square Fish logo designed by Filomena Tuosto

7 9 10 8

AR: 4.8 / LEXILE: 720L

CONTENTS

Lions & Liars

1

The Lion, Gazelle, Meerkat-Butt Theory of Life

FREDERICK FREDERICKSON WAS THINKING ABOUT strawberry daiquiris when the dodgeball slammed into his face.

The pale pink frost, too thick to come up the straw. The toothpick umbrella. The maraschino cherries, speared on a tiny plastic saber.

The delicate cartilage in Frederick's nose *crunched*, and his knees hit the ground.

"*Ahhh!*" he wailed. The vision of the daiquiri vanished, and water sprang into his eyes.

Frederick was ten. He did not cry, but if a dodgeball hit you directly in the nose, your eyes automatically released water. So, when Devin Goodyear came to stand over him, Frederick *wasn't* crying. His eyes were automatically releasing water.

"Jeez, Frederickson." Frederick could tell from the tone of Devin's voice that the other boy was shaking his head.

"You better not tell anyone we were playing dodgeball," Devin warned.

"*I wobe*," Frederick said. He was trying to say *I won't*, but between the automatic release of eye water and the blood pouring out of his nostrils, he sounded like he had a head cold. "*I wobe tell.*"

Frederick was kneeling behind a set of bleachers that blocked him from view of the recess monitors. The students weren't allowed to play dodgeball. Every year the teachers told them the story of how one time, a group of kids had been playing dodgeball, and how Candace Licky had gotten hit in the head so hard that she was knocked unconscious and she fell on the ground, hitting her head a second time, and she didn't die, but she *could've* died, and if any of the students died, the teachers would be in big trouble and lose their jobs. And that was why the kids weren't allowed to play dodgeball.

"Because only a total loser would tell." Devin didn't

sound angry. He wasn't trying to bully Frederick. He was just being informative. Frederick appreciated that.

Devin sighed then and walked away, leaving Frederick's friends, Joel Mincey and Raj Pal, to hook their arms around his elbows and haul him to his feet.

"*I'b fine*," Frederick said in a thick voice, trying to wave them away.

"You're *bleeding*," Raj said. He dropped Frederick's arm and stepped back, wrinkling his nose.

"Come on," Joel said to Raj. "He's got to go to the nurse, and I'm not taking him by myself." He looked over his shoulder, checking to see if anyone was watching them. "Hurry up," he muttered to Frederick. "We look like idiots."

Frederick didn't know why they thought they had to take him to the nurse. "*I'b fine!*" he insisted, wiping at the blood that had dripped on his T-shirt.

By lunchtime, Frederick's nose had swollen until it looked like an ugly, overripe plum hanging off his face. The nurse had given him a Ziploc bag full of ice to hold on it. During the morning lessons, the ice had turned into a bag of water that had sweat all over his worksheets, making them soggy and translucent. The bag now sloshed at the edge of Frederick's lunch tray.

"Why'd you agree to play dodgeball with Devin Goodyear in the first place?" Joel asked as they waited in the lunch line with their trays.

Devin and his friends almost always had a secret dodgeball game going, but Frederick, Raj, and Joel didn't hang out with them. Today, though, Frederick had walked right over and joined in.

"*You* were playing, too," Frederick pointed out in a low voice. He didn't want any of the teachers to overhear them talking about dodgeball.

"Because *you* were," Joel said, rolling his eyes. "I was trying to keep you from getting killed."

Frederick would've snorted, but his nose wasn't up to it. Joel was the least athletic of the three of them, but he always talked big. The way he talked, you would think he had three Super Bowl rings and a medal for saving people from a burning building.

"I don't even like dodgeball," Raj said pensively. "But I didn't know what I would do if the two of you played and I didn't, so I played. I think that means I gave in to peer pressure. That's something I need to work on." Raj was interested in self-improvement. Before his baseball games, all the other players packed their cheeks with gum and went out on the field, looking cool tossing balls in the air. Raj stayed in the dugout, reading statistics about the opposing team and doing alternate nostril breathing.

The three of them slid their trays down the counter. The lunch lady pinched a single barbecued chicken wing with her tongs and dropped it onto Frederick's tray. The wing was so tiny that Frederick thought it must've come off a miniature chicken. Frederick looked from the wing on his tray to the heaping-full serving dish on the other side of the Plexiglas sneeze guard. He raised his eyes up to the lunch lady. The elastic of her hairnet dug a purple line in her forehead. Frederick tried to smile a winning smile at her, but all he managed was a grimace of pain.

"Please, may I have a little more?" He lifted his tray hopefully, tilting it toward her. The melted ice pack sloshed sadly.

Her eyes narrowed. She didn't seem to move a muscle, but the tongs in her hand began to click menacingly. Frederick suddenly had the impression that he was standing across from a giant, angry lobster in a hairnet. He swallowed and moved down the line.

"Today's my birthday," Joel told the lady.

She dropped a single wing on his tray, too, splattering the tray and Joel with specks of barbecue sauce.

"Vegetarian," Raj mumbled, even though he wasn't, and he hurried past her without making eye contact.

They sat at their usual table.

"I wanted to play dodgeball with Devin," Frederick said, getting back to their conversation, "because I want to get better at sports and stuff." He paused. "I want to beat him at something." He said this sentence carefully, in one quick rush of breath, like he was removing a Jenga block from a tower. This was something he'd been thinking about for a while, but he'd never admitted it out loud to Joel or Raj before. He waited now to see how they would react.

Joel snorted through his perfectly working nose.

"What's that supposed to mean?" Frederick asked in annoyance. "I could beat him."

Frederick had never won anything that he could remember. He'd never been *that* guy. That guy who scored goals and won the recess games . . . that guy who got laughs in class and walked through the school like he owned the place. In fact, Frederick was the opposite of *that* guy. He was the one who missed the shot and lost the game for everyone else, the one who got laughed *at*, the one who walked through the school and stepped in spilled Kool-Aid that dried sticky to the bottom of his shoe so that every time he took a step he had to peel his foot off the floor with an embarrassing *sque-e-e-e-lcha*.

Frederick had always been okay with the fact that he was a loser because he'd believed that one day, he would *become* the kind of person everybody wanted to hang out with. Like how the Ugly Duckling became a swan. Or how Harry Potter became a wizard.

But then he had started fifth grade a week ago, and he was still the same old Frederick, and he'd begun to worry. What if he wasn't going to transform into his true awesome self? What if there was some secret to it? Frederick didn't know what the secret was. But he couldn't just sit around waiting anymore. He had to help things along, and he'd decided that the best way to become cool was to beat Devin Goodyear, the coolest guy on Earth.

"You're never going to beat Devin at dodgeball," Joel said, like he was reading Frederick's mind.

"I could win," Frederick argued. "It's a definite possibility."

Joel looked at him for a moment and saw that he was serious. "Oh, *brother*," he drawled.

"Don't 'Oh, brother' me," Frederick said, and he

would've said it in a nasty way, but using any intense tones of voice hurt his nose, so he had to say everything in neutral.

"Look," said Joel, jabbing the straw into his juice box, "it's like this. There are people who are lions, right? Devin's a lion. He's big. He gets all the meat. He can do whatever he wants. Then there are people who are gazelles." He slurped his juice, making his cheeks deflate.

"Are you saying I'm a gazelle?" Frederick tried to think of an animal that was even lower than a gazelle so that he could tell Joel, *Oh, I'm a gazelle, huh? Well then, you're a . . .*

"I'd say you and I are more like meerkats," Raj said as he pulled the soft middle out of a roll. "No." He looked up and frowned into the distance. "We're more like fleas. We're the fleas that are biting the butt of a meerkat."

Frederick opened his mouth to answer, but—

"Joel's not as low down as a flea," Raj continued, lost in his thoughts. "He's something like a hyena. But he's the hyena that none of the other hyenas like."

"There's no shame in being the flea," Joel said to Frederick.

"I'm *not* the flea," Frederick snapped.

Joel pointed his chicken wing at Frederick. "You need to accept the fact that life is going to be horrible for you. You're not going to win at dodgeball. You're not going to get extra chicken. You're never going to be as cool as Devin Goodyear."

"That's not true," Frederick said. "You don't know the future. Maybe I'll win the lottery. Maybe I'll be president one day."

Raj blinked at him. "That's very unlikely."

"I know it's unlikely," Frederick said. "But my point is that anything could happen."

"But it's not *likely* to happen," Raj insisted, as if Frederick was being stupid.

"I *just* said that!" Frederick said. "I just said that I knew it wasn't likely, so why are you telling me again?"

"The chances of you winning the lottery are one in a million." Raj patted his paper napkin against the corner of his mouth. "Or maybe a hundred million. Actually, I'm just making those numbers up. It's probably not an even number like that. It's probably something like one in three hundred forty-two million three hundred and two."

"That's still an even number," Joel said. "Because it ends with a two."

"*Please*, will you stop it?" Frederick said moodily. He poked the wobbly Ziploc bag of water that had been an ice pack.

"Hey, Dev!" Joel called.

Frederick looked up sharply.

Devin was walking past them toward his own table, but he slowed and came over. Devin was Frederick's height, which was average, but while Frederick was very skinny, Devin was stocky and strong. He had red hair, and he always wore a crooked smile, like he had a great secret and he wasn't letting anyone in on it.

Although, thought Frederick, maybe it wasn't such a secret. Maybe he was smiling now because his tray was loaded with barbecued chicken. Barbecued chicken stuck out over the sides of the tray. About fifteen barbecued chickens were stacked on it.

"I was just explaining the theory of life to Frederick," Joel said, eyeing the chicken.

"Shut up, Joel," Frederick muttered, looking down at his own puny lunch, but Joel was already going on.

"How there are people who are lions and people who are gazelles and people who are fleas on meerkat butts." Joel paused, waiting for Devin to give some sign that he was following along.

Frederick glanced up from his green beans.

Devin's easy smile didn't falter. "I'm the lion," he said.

"Exactly." Joel snapped his fingers and pointed at Devin.

Devin shifted his tray so that he was holding it with one hand. Probably he was just showing off that he was able to hold the heavy tray with one hand—there was no other reason not to hold it with two hands. "Who's the flea?" he asked. He looked at Frederick. "Are you the flea?"

"I'm *not* the flea." Frederick put as much conviction in his voice as he could.

"There's nothing wrong with being the flea," Devin said. "Every animal plays its part."

"I'm not the flea!" It stung, hearing Joel and Raj and Devin say he was a flea. Frederick had always felt like he was a loser, and he had sometimes *worried* that everyone else thought he was one, too. But he'd hoped that maybe it was just something *he* knew and that no one else thought of him that way.

"Okay, you're not the flea." Devin shrugged in a *suit yourself* way.

Frederick sighed. "*Thank* you."

"But if you *were* . . . ," Devin said, "it wouldn't make you any less important." He winked at Frederick.

"Hey, Dev!" a boy's voice called. It was Lucas Washington, one of Devin's friends, sitting at their lunch table. He was twisted in his chair, turned around to see where Devin was and what was taking him so long. Lucas beckoned with his arm. "Come on, Dev!" he called.

"Gotta go," Devin said, giving Frederick, Raj, and Joel another shrug.

Then he prowled away to his own table and the boys who waited there and the entire flock of dead barbecued chickens they were gnawing on. Frederick watched them a moment longer.

It sounded embarrassing and stupid, even in Frederick's head, but what he really wanted—what he'd always wanted—was for someone to wave him over like Lucas had just waved Devin over. He wanted a friend who liked him so much that they wanted to hang out with him. A friend who, when they realized he wasn't around, would find him and beckon him over. *Come on, Frederick.*

Raj and Joel were okay friends, and Frederick knew he should be happy that he had friends at all. Beggars couldn't be choosers. But Raj was way more interested in baseball and his grades than he was in being Frederick's friend. And Joel only cared about himself. If Frederick was slow getting to his lunch table, Raj and Joel wouldn't wave him over. They would just keep eating and forget all about him. But if he could beat Devin at dodgeball, then maybe they'd treat him better.

That was what it really meant to be the lion, to be Devin, to be *that* guy.

Frederick turned his attention back to his own table and found that Joel was watching him with a smirk, like he guessed the pathetic things Frederick was thinking.

Frederick's ears got hot. "What about my vacation?" he said, trying to distract Joel. "What about that?"

Joel and Raj exchanged a look.

"That's why I got hit with the ball," Frederick said.

"I could've won, but I wasn't paying attention. I was thinking about my vacation."

Every fall, the week of Labor Day, Frederick's family went on a cruise. It was the best week of Frederick's year, and today . . . today was the Friday before Labor Day weekend. It was the one undeniably cool thing about Frederick. He had been on *six* cruises in his life. Most kids his age hadn't even been on one.

"How can I be a flea," Frederick went on, "when I'm about to spend seven days on a cruise ship with strawberry daiquiris whenever I want them?"

"You know they're not *real* daiquiris, right?" Joel said.

"And a midnight buffet," Frederick went on, "with a—"

"Chocolate fountain," Raj and Joel said together in resigned voices.

"Exactly," Frederick said, picking up his chicken wing and biting it, talking with his mouth full. "And world-class—"

"Entertainment," Joel said.

"And fresh—"

"Ocean air," Raj finished for him. "Please stop it."

"I'm not going to stop it," Frederick said, "because

clearly you've both forgotten that I'm leaving tonight to catch my boat to go on *my* vacation."

"The vacation that you're missing my birthday party for," Joel said with a frown.

"Exactly," Frederick said, glad that he had the chance to get one on Joel after Joel had called Frederick a flea. "*That* vacation. I'm just saying, your theory of life is wrong because sometimes things *do* go my way." Frederick tried to take another bite of his chicken wing, but his teeth closed on clean bone. The meat was gone.

"Things never go your way," Joel said.

"They will for the next seven days," Frederick said, trying to get the last word in.

Joel leaned over the table toward him. "Wanna bet?"

2

Hurricane Hernando

"I'VE NEVER EVEN *HEARD* OF HURRICANE HERNANDO," Frederick said later that afternoon.

"That's because you don't watch the news," Sarah Anne said. "Because you're so self-involved that you don't care about the world around you."

Sarah Anne was Frederick's big sister. She was thirteen, and she was self-righteous. The two of them stood in the living room. The Weather Channel was on full blast, and Sarah Anne was explaining why their parents had decided to cancel the vacation at the last minute. Apparently, it had something to do with a storm spiraling in the Atlantic.

"Hurricane *Hernando*?" Frederick repeated,

putting his hands on top of his head and gazing at the TV in dismay. "But we're supposed to have our vacation. I *need* my vacation." He'd been looking forward to his vacation for weeks. It was like there was a strawberry daiquiri sitting on a table in the middle of the desert. And he'd been crawling toward it, dehydrated, and he'd just made it to the table only to realize it was a mirage.

"Oh, yes, that's obviously the important thing here," Sarah Anne said, her voice rising. "I'm sure the people who are evacuating their homes and hoping they don't die are worried about Frederick Frederickson missing his *vacation*."

"Are you being funny?" Frederick said, lowering his arms and turning to look at her.

Sarah Anne perched on the edge of the coffee table and crossed her legs. "*Obviously*," she said.

"Because your face makes it hard to tell," Frederick said.

Sarah Anne sprang up. She grabbed his ears and pulled him so close he could see her tonsils as she yelled, "What's wrong with my face?"

Mrs. Frederickson came into the living room carrying the yellow emergency flashlight.

"Don't grab his head," she snapped, and shooed Sarah Anne out of the way. "He's injured." She clicked the light on and pointed it into Frederick's eyes, grabbing his chin so he couldn't squirm away.

"Hold still, Freddie," she said. "I'm checking to see if your pupils dilate. That blow could've given you a concussion."

"The nurse at school already did that." Frederick squinted.

His mom pointed the beam away from him so he could see her. "Really?" she asked.

He nodded.

"Huh." She tapped his chest with the light. "I knew that was a good school." Then she headed back to the kitchen to put the flashlight away. Frederick followed, right on her heels. Sarah Anne followed *him*, right on *his* heels.

"I think you're making a bad decision," he told his mom.

"Okay," Mrs. Frederickson said, not looking back at him.

"Okay?" Frederick repeated.

"Okay, I heard you," Mrs. Frederickson said. "You think Dad and I are making a bad decision." She stuffed the flashlight in the Thing Drawer. "But you're wrong. We're not going. You need to get over it." She closed the drawer.

Sarah Anne leaned against the kitchen counter and crossed her arms, smirking at Frederick.

Frederick tugged his bloodstained T-shirt straight and shot an *I loathe every atom of your being* face at his sister, before ignoring her. He was going to have to be careful here, reasoning with his mom.

Frederick knew—in an intellectual way—that his mom loved him and Sarah Anne. But being loved by her was like being loved by a bear. And not like a teddy bear or Pooh Bear. More like a grizzly bear. One that had just gotten its paw caught in a trap and was tearing through the forest, looking for a hunter it could rip to shreds.

"*Mo-o-o-m,*" Frederick said, but he snapped his mouth closed. He had heard the beginnings of a whine in his voice. Ten-year-olds did *not* whine. He took a deep breath and *explained*, in a calm voice. "I've just been looking forward to this vacation for a really, really, really, really, really long time," he said. "It's been a bad day. A bad, *bad* day, and I need to go on vacation." He folded his hands together prayerfully. "I need a daiquiri in the worst kind of way."

"You and me both, kiddo," his mom said.

She opened the refrigerator and peered inside. The refrigerator that had a note magneted to it. A note with a list of all the last-minute things they needed to lock, check, and turn off tonight before they got in the car with their suitcases. It was also the refrigerator that only had pickle spears, horseradish, and Cokes in it, because that morning, Frederick's dad had trashed everything that would spoil while they were away for a week.

Mrs. Frederickson slammed the refrigerator shut without taking anything out. "But we don't need to get caught in a hurricane," she said with a sigh.

"It might not even hit us," Frederick said.

"It's not pointing directly at Port Verde Shoals," his mom admitted. "But storms can turn without warning."

"Probably the weather people are exaggerating," Frederick reasoned. "It might not be a bad storm."

"Category Five," Sarah Anne said under her breath. "Frederick wants to drown us all."

"I'm not worried about drowning so much as

getting really seasick," Mrs. Frederickson said, wrinkling her nose.

"*Gah!*" Sarah Anne stomped her foot. "Don't you think it's pretty selfish of you to worry about getting nauseous when there are people who are evacuating—"

"The word you're looking for is *nauseated*," their mom said. "And you're being self-righteous, which is *nauseous*."

"I am *not*," Sarah Anne said. "I'm—"

"Sarah Anne," Mrs. Fredrickson interrupted in a mild voice, her eyebrows lifting in feigned surprise. "You are being very"—she paused a moment, and the air in the kitchen seemed to crackle—"*un*attractive," Mrs. Frederickson finished.

Sarah Anne paled.

Ever since she'd become a teenager, Sarah Anne was obsessed with how she looked. If someone told her that her left arm was unattractive, she'd probably chop it off.

"I am not," Sarah Anne said in a strangled voice. "I am not being unattractive."

Unattractive red splotches erupted on her neck.

"*I'm* trying to do the right thing. *I'm* being a good

person. And—and neither one of you appreciates me!" Sarah Anne whirled around and fled.

"On the bright side," Mrs. Frederickson said cheerfully, as if she had a perfectly normal daughter, "you can go to Joel's birthday party now."

It took Frederick a moment to understand what she was talking about.

"I don't want to go to Joel's birthday," he grumped.

"Yeah, I don't either," his mom said, grabbing her key ring off the counter and looping it around her finger. "But it's dinnertime, and I'm hungry, and I bet Joel's family has food."

Frederick looked around the kitchen, panicked. He didn't want to see *Joel*. Not now, when Joel had told him he was a flea. Not now, when he was supposed to be in the backseat of the family's car on the way to Port Verde Shoals. Not when he'd told Joel he was missing his party to go on vacation.

"Sarah Anne!" Mrs. Frederickson yelled. "Get ready to go! We're taking your brother to a party so we can get burgers!"

"Couldn't you just . . ." Frederick waved his arms, indicating the stove, the fridge, the oven. "*Cook* something?"

Slowly, his mom turned to face him. Her eyes focused on him, and she seemed to be stretching taller and taller, filling up the entire kitchen.

"That thing you just said," she growled. "Why don't you say it again?"

3

And Then It Came Unattached

A GREASY, SIZZLING BURGER PLOPPED ONTO THE PAPER plate Frederick was holding. Joel's dad pointed the spatula at it and declared, "That there'll put hair on your chest."

Frederick looked from the brown meat patty to the curly chest hairs blooming from the neck of Mr. Mincey's chef's apron.

Joel's favorite rap song was bumping out of the portable speaker set up on the patio. Mr. Mincey was waiting for Frederick to respond, but chest hair didn't seem like the kind of thing you were supposed to discuss. Of course, Frederick wouldn't *have* to discuss it if he had been on his way to Port Verde Shoals right now.

"*Uhh* . . . thank you," Frederick said to Mr. Mincey, and turned away to carry his burger to some private part of the Minceys' yard, where he could dig a small hole and bury it and then dig a larger hole and crawl into it and die.

"Hey, what happened to your face?" Mr. Mincey called after him.

Frederick pretended not to hear.

The Minceys' back patio was full of people. There were Joel's aunts and uncles and cousins and grandparents and step-grandparents and a great-grandma, who was bundled in several sweaters and tucked in a lawn chair. Frederick wove through the clusters of conversation, steering clear of his mom, who was holding a burger in one hand and a Coke in the other and chatting animatedly with Mrs. Mincey. He didn't make it out of the crowd to enact his burger-burying plan before Joel and Raj found him.

"There's my best buddy!" Joel crowed. He threw an arm around Frederick and squeezed him. "I knew my best buddy wouldn't miss my birthday party!"

"Cut it out," Frederick said, trying to shrug Joel

off his shoulders without his burger sliding off his plate. "And stop calling me your buddy."

"But aren't you supposed to be on your way somewhere?" Joel asked in mock confusion. With his free hand he tapped his finger against his chin, and then a smile broke over his face. "Oh, *yeah*," he said. "You're supposed to be going on a cruise, aren't you? With a chocolate fountain. And world-class entertainment."

"Fresh ocean air," Raj said, tilting his head back and raising his arms dramatically to the sky. "Ice-cold daiquiris."

"'S'not funny," Frederick mumbled.

"Snot *is* funny," Joel and Raj said automatically.

"Seriously, though," Joel said. He let go of Frederick, and the smile slid off his face. "I feel bad about your vacation. And I have something for you."

"You do?" Frederick said, knowing full well that Joel didn't have anything for him. Joel never had anything for him, and besides, it was Joel's birthday, which meant that people gave things to Joel, not the other way around.

"Come on," Joel said. "Follow me."

Frederick had a bad feeling. Actually, it wasn't a *feeling* at all. It was a certainty. Frederick was certain that Joel had something mean or stupid in mind and that the whole point of the mean, stupid thing was to make Frederick unhappy so that Joel could be amused. And yet . . . Frederick found himself following Joel and Raj with his rapidly cooling burger patty.

Later, if someone asked Frederick *why* he had followed his friends to his mean, stupid, not-good fate, he would've given them not one, but two answers: (1) He couldn't think of anything better to do, and (2) *Eh*, why not?

Joel led Raj and Frederick away from the party and the music to the edge of his yard. He took them down the short hill that led to the river.

The river was the Omigoshee. The water was dark and cold and banked with white sand. Gnarled trees with twisting limbs stretched out over the water. Whenever Frederick wanted to go swimming or fishing, he had to get his dad to take him to the public parking area, and he had to use the public section of the river where fifteen other boys and their dads were doing the same thing. And all the boys had cooler swim trunks than Frederick's, which had tugboats on them, and all their dads had bigger trucks than Mr. Frederickson, who didn't have a truck at all—he had a Corolla. But Joel and his dad, they had their own private section of the river.

They also had their own floating wooden dock that extended into the Omigoshee, and Joel led Raj and Frederick onto this dock and stopped. At the end of the dock was Mr. Mincey's small white fishing boat with its shiny black motor. The motor was up out of the water. The lines tying the boat to the dock were pulled taut.

Joel threw out his arm toward the boat like he was presenting Frederick with something fantastic. His mouth curved in a smile.

"What is it?" Frederick asked suspiciously. Obviously it was a boat, but he wasn't taking any chances.

"It's your own private cruise!" Joel exclaimed in delight. "Sail away and enjoy your chocolate fountain!" Then he burst into loud, braying donkey laughs.

Frederick worked to keep his face expressionless

and not show Joel his annoyance. "That's not even funny," he said.

Raj rubbed the back of his neck. "It's really *not* funny," he said, turning to Joel. "Why is it funny?"

Joel stopped laughing. His face shone with sweat. The music from the party drifted, tinny and distant, to the river, and a mosquito zinged around Frederick's head.

"You need to get your sense of humor checked out," Joel said, shaking his head.

"My sense of humor is fine," Frederick answered. "I'm just sick of you acting like I'm some kind of reject."

"Well, let's look at the facts," Joel began.

"Your theory of life is stupid," Frederick cut him off, his voice rising.

"Have you got a better one?" Joel demanded.

"Yeah!" Frederick said. "You just want to think I'm a loser because *you're* a loser," he said recklessly, wanting to show Joel that he'd had enough of Joel picking on him. The effect would've been better if he could've waved his arms around and gotten up in Joel's face, but he couldn't do that because he might drop his burger. So all he could do was stand there, holding his paper plate, his hands shaking with anger. "I'm not a loser," he said, his burger patty trembling. "I'm awesome. And I'm great. And I'm going to do awesome, great things and I don't care what you do!"

Frederick didn't actually believe he was awesome or great. But he could sense that this was the moment in the movie when the hero took a stand. This was where he showed them what he was made of. Frederick needed to sound tough here.

"So this is my cruise, huh?" Frederick said, his voice cracking. "You're giving this to me?"

Raj shrugged at him.

Then Frederick stepped off the dock and into the boat. Holding his plate in one hand, he snatched off one of the lines that secured the boat to the dock and sat right down on the metal seat. He balanced his plate on his knees. Then he reached backward and awkwardly shook off the second line.

"Thanks a lot," he said when he'd gotten it off. "And tell your dad I said thanks, too." Frederick shoved against the dock, and the boat drifted away, the current pulling the bow gently. "I hope he doesn't mind that you gave away his boat."

He looked up at his friends standing on the dock, and he smiled and spread his hands wide. "What are you going to do now?" he asked.

Raj and Joel stared at him. Their faces were blank, like Frederick had finally, at last, completely stumped them. Then . . .

"What are *you* gonna do now?" Joel asked.

Frederick looked down at the widening gap of water between the boat and the dock. The current had already carried him out into the river and was easing him downstream.

"*Ahh*, shoot," Frederick said, and he reached out for the dock. His fingertips brushed the edge, but he couldn't grab on. He tried again, but he was too far out. His heart flopped like a fish out of water, gasping for air . . . or gasping for water or for . . . whatever.

Joel and Raj went to the edge of the dock and looked down at Frederick.

"What *are* you going to do?" Raj asked. "You know this isn't really a cruise ship, right?" He was speaking in a slow, careful voice, as if he was afraid that Frederick was losing touch with reality.

"Wow," Joel said sarcastically. "I guess you really

showed me." But even as he spoke, he was kneeling at the edge of the dock and leaning forward, stretching out his hand toward Frederick.

"Grab," he said.

Frederick reached as far as he could without overturning the boat. His fingertips touched Joel's, but then they moved apart, out of reach.

Joel wobbled for a moment, almost falling face-first into the river. He snatched his arm back and balanced himself. He shook his head. "Okay," he said, "this is going to be fine. Drop the motor in the water. Then I'll tell you how to start it. It's really easy."

Frederick's hands were sweaty as he moved toward the back of the boat. He hadn't used the motor before. And he'd never paid attention when Mr. Mincey had been revving it up.

He saw a lever that he thought he'd seen Mr. Mincey use to lower the propeller into the water. Frederick pulled it.

A bolt dropped and *clanged* against the boat's bottom. The heavy motor tipped over the edge with a solid *thud*. And then it came unattached and splashed into the water. It sank and was gone.

"Ahh!" Frederick yelled. He looked down at his shadowy reflection wavering in the dark water and then up at the dock.

Joel was on his knees, staring at him in horror. Raj was holding his head in both hands like he was trying to keep it from falling off his shoulders.

"Ahh!" Frederick yelled again, grabbing the sides of the boat as the river pulled him away from his friends.

"I said drop it in the water!" Joel yelled. "I didn't say *drop* it in the water!"

"That's the same thing!" Frederick yelled back. "It's literally the same thing!"

"It *is* literally the same thing!" Raj shouted.

"Okay!" Joel said. "Okay, okay! *Uh* . . . Drop the anchor!" He grabbed the edge of the dock and leaned as far forward as he could, as if he would reach out and throw the anchor himself. "Drop the anchor!"

Frederick looked around frantically and spotted the small anchor in the bottom of the boat. He dove for it, not caring how the boat rocked and dipped. He hauled the anchor up onto the seat.

"Do you want me to drop it in the water, or

am I supposed to *drop* it in the water?" he shouted sarcastically, and threw the anchor over the side. The anchor disappeared into the river, and Frederick felt a moment of relief. Then he realized the trees on the riverbank were still sliding by. "What . . ."

"The line!" Joel cried. "Why isn't the anchor tied off to the line?"

Frederick looked down and saw the rope, which was supposed to be tied to the anchor, neatly coiled in the bottom.

"*Gah!*" he yelled.

Raj was still holding his head on his shoulders, turning it so that he could watch Frederick move farther down the river. "We need to get someone who knows more about boats," he said to Joel. "We need to get someone who knows about rivers. We need—"

"Just jump!" Joel yelled, ignoring Raj and getting to his feet. He hopped up and down on the dock. "Forget the boat! Just jump."

Frederick stood. The boat swayed under his feet, and he steadied himself. This was going to be lousy. His clothes would be wet. His mom would be mad. He'd have to tell Mr. Mincey what had happened to his motor. And his anchor. And his boat. But he didn't have a choice. His legs tensed.

Then Raj screamed. He screamed high and shrill, and it was such an un-Raj-like sound that Frederick forgot what he was doing and stared at his friend. Raj didn't scream. He stated opinions and observations in a dry voice.

But now Raj was screaming and jabbing a finger at the river.

Frederick looked down where Raj was pointing and saw a dark log floating in the water, moving up alongside the boat.

"Wait," said Frederick. "Is that . . ."

"Alligator!" Joel yelled. "Gator! Gator! Gator!"

Frederick snatched up the burger patty from the bottom of the boat, drew back his arm, and hurled it at the alligator. It hit the gator's armored neck, bounced off, and *plooped* into the water. The alligator didn't blink.

Then the giant tail swished through the water, rocking the boat. Frederick lost his footing and landed on his butt on the metal seat. A jolt rocketed up his spine.

He tore his eyes away from the alligator to look up at his friends and found that the river had carried him so far downstream that Raj and Joel looked quite small. Their voices carried to him across the distance.

Joel grabbed Raj's neck and shook. "Get help!" he yelled in Raj's face. "Get help! Get help!"

Then Frederick saw someone scrambling down the hill toward the river. The person was running along the riverbank, trying to catch up with the boat. Frederick squinted.

"Oh, brother," he said, and groaned.

It was Sarah Anne.

Sarah Anne ran until she reached the edge of the Minceys' property and the ten-foot-tall chain-link fence that kept trespassers off their land. Frederick expected her to stop then and turn back, but she launched herself at the fence, catching it halfway up. The fence shivered under her weight as she scaled it.

Frederick stared. Sarah Anne was moving like freaking Jason Bourne. She grabbed the top of the fence and swung herself over, dropping to the ground and landing in a crouch. Then she was off again, moving parallel to the boat, hurdling over logs and plowing through briars and bushes.

Whoa, Frederick thought. Sarah Anne was . . . awesome. She didn't look like Frederick's self-righteous big sister at all. She looked like an action hero—heroine—arms pumping, blond hair streaming behind her, eyes bright as sparklers.

Unfortunately, the Omigoshee, which seemed so sluggish from the shore, was faster moving than Frederick had ever realized. And Sarah Anne, despite slapping willow branches out of her path like a human weed whacker, was falling farther and farther behind.

"Stop!" Sarah Anne's voice shouted through the foliage. "Frederick, you stop right now!" she commanded. As if Frederick had the power to stop the boat and guide it back to his sister but was choosing not to.

The alligator's tail swished again. It was swimming along with the boat. Its rough skin scraped the hull. Frederick clenched his arms to his sides and pinched his knees together, positioning himself in the absolute center of the metal seat, not wanting a single morsel of flesh to be any closer to the gator than it had to be.

"Sarah Anne!" he called wildly.

And then Mr. Mincey's boat went around a bend, and Frederick was completely alone.

4

Are You There, God?
It's Me, Frederick

"OKAY, GOD," FREDERICK SAID, PEERING AHEAD AT A jagged stump that jutted out from the riverbank and stretched over the water. "If, by the time we reach that stump, someone comes and rescues me, I'll give every penny of my college savings account to the Hurricane Hernando victims."

Gradually, the stump came into better focus as Frederick drew nearer.

He waited for some kind of sign—people crashing through the woods and yelling, *We're here, son!*—but none came. The boat slid past the jagged stump with a ripple.

Frederick squinted ahead as far as he could. The

light was fading—the light had been fading for a while now, but he was trying to pretend it was still daytime.

"If, by the time we reach that bit of Spanish moss hanging there, I'm saved, I'll . . . ," Frederick thought. "I'll never say another bad word as long as I live."

An hour or so before, when Frederick had first started talking to God, he had been very formal about it: *Dearest heavenly Father, please help me in this, my hour of need* and all that. But as the light had faded and no help had come and the boat had slid past *that* stump and *that* weird bit of sand and *that* tree that looked like Elvis Presley, he had gotten more and more casual. His Sunday school teacher was always saying you could talk to God just like you would a friend. Of course, Frederick had never gotten much help from his friends, either.

He looked up as he glided beneath the Spanish moss. "Okay," he said in a tired voice. "Fine. I guess I've got absolutely nothing you want."

Being in a boat, alone, floating down the Omigoshee as the night set in, was 50 percent scary—blood-chilling, goose-bump-raising scary. The alligator had sunk under the water ages ago, but it could still be down there, just beneath Frederick, because alligators could hold their breath for a long time. Probably.

Frederick didn't actually know, but probably they could because alligators seemed to be awesome at everything. So, it was 50 percent scary.

And it was 10 percent exciting. The only times Frederick had been in a boat before were when he was on a cruise (and that didn't feel like being on a real boat) and when he was riding with Joel and his dad, which wasn't often. It was kind of nice to get to have the boat all to himself for a change, without Joel reminding him that it didn't belong to him.

The other 40 percent of the experience was . . . well . . . boring. As Frederick passed the six hundred thousandth tree, he regretted throwing his burger patty at the alligator. He would've eaten it now, even though it would've been cold and he didn't have a bun or mayonnaise and it might've put hair on his chest.

Frederick pulled his T-shirt up and inspected his thin chest to see if there were any hairs there. He didn't think so, but it was hard to see in the darkness.

He sighed and tugged his shirt down. He gingerly touched his enormous nose and winced.

Maybe Joel and Raj and Devin were right. Maybe he *was* just a flea, and he was always going to be a flea because that was the way the world worked.

Let's look at the facts, Joel had said, and Frederick did. He had lost at dodgeball. He'd broken his nose. He hadn't gotten to go on his cruise—the one thing he'd been looking forward to for weeks. When his parents found him, he was going to be in trouble for losing Mr. Mincey's motor. And his anchor. His friends were never going to like him enough to wave him over and say, *Come on, Frederick.*

Those were all things he couldn't have . . . because he was a flea. He guessed he should go ahead and get used to it. Try to make the best of it.

Frederick crawled into the bottom of the boat and pulled his knees in, curling up like a roly-poly right before a shoe squished it. He folded his hands under his cheek so that his face wouldn't touch the cold metal. He closed his eyes and tried to imagine a strawberry daiquiri, but couldn't.

Owls hooted, and crickets trilled, and water swashed and slopped against the boat's hull. As he

lay in the bottom of the boat, Frederick did not cry. His eyes didn't even automatically release water.

He just wished someone was there with him to notice that he didn't cry.

Frederick woke in the night and realized the boat had stopped. He sat up. The boat's nose was stuck on the sandy bank; Frederick had finally run ashore. He sank back down in relief.

The next time he woke up, it was morning. Frederick pushed his hair out of his eyes. He was alone at the edge of the river. The boat rocked beneath him but didn't dislodge itself from the sand. He smelled pancakes and coffee and then heard a man's angry voice crackle through a loudspeaker: "Move it, maggots! Pick up your name tag and report to the welcome meeting ASAP!"

5

Dashiell Blackwood

FREDERICK SCRAMBLED OUT OF THE BOAT AND ONTO the riverbank as gracefully as a one-legged crab that had been hit in the head with a mallet.

The bottom of the boat hadn't been the most comfortable place to sleep. Frederick's legs had cramped and gone numb. He had a crick in his neck, and he had pulled something in his shoulder. But none of that mattered, because he smelled pancakes.

Mr. Mincey's boat had landed at the base of a weeping willow tree. The trailing fronds tickled Frederick's neck as he dragged the boat farther onto the sand. He gripped the edge of the boat and leaned back, straining with all his weight. The boat slid an inch. He didn't want it drifting down the river; it was bad enough that he'd lost the motor and the anchor. At least he could tell Mr. Mincey he hadn't lost his boat. When Frederick was too exhausted to haul it any farther, he left it and lurched away from the water.

In the distance, the man's voice barked over the loudspeaker again. "Pick up your name tag before the meeting. BEFORE the meeting!"

Frederick emerged over the edge of the riverbank and straightened up, pressing his hands into his lower back, his spine cracking like a glow stick.

"Pancakes," he said, looking around.

He was in a forest, but there were signs of civilization. Through the trees, he saw a school bus parked in a paved drive. It was far away, but Frederick saw that the name of the school district had been blacked out with paint. A stream of boys trickled off the bus and gathered around a table set up beneath a flagpole. They called out to one another and laughed. One boy grabbed the flagpole and started to climb it.

Beyond the boys were a large log building and a cluster of smaller buildings with green tin roofs.

Between Frederick and the buildings, slightly off to the side, stood a big, open tent. Under the tent there were mismatched tables and folding chairs and a gray-haired lady who was setting up several steel serving trays.

Frederick's eyes fixed on the serving trays. He started limping toward the tent as fast as he could, tripping over pine roots and stomping through ant beds, not caring if he was walking through poison ivy or nests of rattlesnakes. When he made it to the tent, he weaved around the tables. His toe caught a chair leg, and he went over, landing on his knees in the cool grass. He crawled to the food table and pulled himself up.

"My stars," the gray-haired woman behind the serving trays said, raising sharp eyebrows at him. "You're supposed to be at the welcome meeting."

Frederick hobbled sideways until he reached the first tray. He lifted off the steel lid and let out a pleased cry as steam wafted into his eyes. Three rows of pancakes, with not a single one missing. They were soft, golden, and round. Frederick's stomach moaned like a humpback whale. He grabbed the first one and bit into it, closing his eyes.

"Don't use your hands!" The woman wrenched the lid out of Frederick's grip and clapped it down protectively over the pancakes.

The pancake was warm and chewy, faintly sweet with a tang of buttermilk. Frederick realized that the last time he'd eaten anything was lunch yesterday when he'd had a roll, some green beans, and one barbecued chicken wing.

The woman's expression softened. "Poor thing." She shook her head. "You were about to starve to death, weren't you?"

"*Muh-huh*," Frederick agreed with his mouth full.

"I'm Miss Betty," the woman said. "I'm just volunteering today for the welcome breakfast. I won't be around the rest of the weekend. Here . . ."

She lifted the lid on a second serving dish, revealing a tower of sausage links. She used the tongs to pull two out and drop them into Frederick's hand. He wrapped the rest of his pancake around the sausages and stuffed the whole thing in his mouth.

"You might get in trouble if the counselors catch you eating your breakfast early," Miss Betty warned.

Frederick's mouth was too full to explain to her that it didn't matter if he ate breakfast early or not.

When you had just survived a terrifying ordeal, you didn't have to follow the rules.

"*And* you're missing the welcome meeting." She shook her head. "You're not off to a good start."

"These are the best things I ever ate in my life," he said, casting a wistful gaze at the pancake tray.

Miss Betty beamed. "*Gah*—all right then," she said. "Have another."

Frederick got another. This time he used the tongs, wanting to show Miss Betty that he was the kind of person who normally used tongs—that earlier he'd just been in a hunger-induced state of frenzy.

Miss Betty watched him closely as he ate, her gaze moving from his head to his toes and back again. Her eyes narrowed suspiciously as they moved over his face. "I'm just a volunteer," she said again. "But I'm going to warn you right now . . ." Her voice turned stern. "There's no fighting at Camp Omigoshee."

"M'okay," Frederick said with his mouth full.

"I mean it," Miss Betty said.

Frederick shrugged and crammed another pancake into his mouth. "M'o*kay*," he said again. He had never been in a fight in his life, and he didn't plan on *ever* being in one if he could help it. So if these people had a rule against fighting, that was fine by him. Then he realized what Miss Betty had called the place.

"Camp?" He looked around. The log cabins, the trees, the school bus that had brought all the boys. This was a camp. Of course it was!

He'd never been to camp before, but Sarah Anne had. She had done archery and gone swimming in lakes and eaten s'mores by a real campfire.

"Camp Omigoshee," Miss Betty said, nodding. "Where boys are *transformed*," she added in a dramatic voice, like she was quoting a slogan. Then she chuckled.

Frederick scrubbed his hands clean on the legs of his shorts and looked around.

Golden sunbeams slanted through the trees. Birds chittered and twittered above. The smell of pancakes and cut grass perfumed the air, and in front of the main log cabin, the American flag billowed majestically against a blue sky.

"*There* you are!" said a voice.

Frederick turned to see a beaming young man stepping under the food tent. He was wearing a baby-blue polo shirt and enormous khaki shorts that would've fit someone five times bigger than him. Around his neck was a lanyard. The lanyard had a badge that showed a handwritten number thirteen.

"Hi! I'm Benjamin," the man said brightly. "I'm your counselor."

Benjamin thrust out his fist, which was clutching a lanyard that matched his own. A name badge twirled at the end of it.

Frederick stared at the lanyard, not understanding what Benjamin the Counselor was expecting him to do with it.

"Oh. *Ahh.*" Benjamin's cheeks turned pink. "You didn't pick this up." He pointed at the badge he was holding. "It was the last one left. And you aren't at the meeting!" he exclaimed. "Why aren't you at the meeting?"

"I was just . . . talking to Miss Betty." Frederick glanced at Miss Betty, who was arranging the pancakes back into perfection.

"*Miss Betty,*" Benjamin said plaintively, turning to her. "He's missed the welcome meeting. That's step one of the campers' transformation process!"

Campers. Benjamin thought Frederick was a

camper. He thought Frederick was supposed to be here.

Miss Betty rolled her eyes, and Benjamin turned away from her and held the lanyard out to Frederick again.

Frederick hesitated.

He knew that now was the moment to explain who he was and what had happened so that Miss Betty and Benjamin could get him back home . . . where he belonged.

But Frederick didn't want to go back. Back home, he was a flea. Back home, nobody liked him.

And then an idea came into Frederick's mind, an idea that made his skin tingle like Coke bubbles. Maybe this camp was the opportunity he'd been waiting for his whole life. Maybe this was his chance to start over and become the person he was supposed to be. Maybe the hurricane and the boat motor falling off had all been for a reason.

He was scared, afraid of the idea that was forming in his mind. But then he knew, with a certainty that shocked him, that if he went back home now, he'd be the same old Frederick forever, and that was even scarier than what he was about to do.

"Thanks." Frederick drew in a deep breath and took the lanyard out of Benjamin's hand. He could hear blood rushing in his ears. His hands trembled with nerves, fear, and hope as he turned the badge over to look at the name. *Dashiell Blackwood.* "Dashiell Blackwood?" He hoped he was pronouncing it right. "That sounds made up," he muttered. He looked up at Benjamin. "But it's not," he said quickly, pulling the lanyard over his head and adjusting the badge so that it faced out. He gave a shaky laugh. "'Cause that's my name."

6

Nosebleed, the Professor, Specs, and Ant Bite

THE NUMBER THIRTEEN WAS WRITTEN IN MARKER ON the back of Frederick's name tag, too.

"That's your group," Benjamin said, following Frederick's gaze. "I'm Group Thirteen's counselor." He tapped his own badge, then glanced down and flipped it over so it showed his name. *Benjamin Merkel, Counselor. Willemon University, Home and Family Science.* "So if you need anything or if you have any questions," Benjamin said, "or if you just want a buddy to talk to, *I*"—he pointed at himself— "am here for *you*." He pointed at Frederick.

"Okay," Frederick said. He hoped there would be s'mores at some point.

"I've been to training," Benjamin confided with a nod. "So I can deal with any problem you might have. Any problem at all."

"'Kay," Frederick said. S'mores were probably more of an afternoon activity. Or maybe even a nighttime activity. Probably the counselors were going to say s'mores were a dessert so they had to be eaten after dinner, but technically that wasn't true, because s'mores could be a dessert *or* a snack. Cake was sort of similar. Cake could be dessert. Or, if it was coffee cake, it could be breakfast. Really there were a lot of—

"I . . . *umm* . . ."

Frederick looked up. Benjamin's cheeks were pink again. He hooked his thumbs through his belt loops and took a deep breath that swelled his stomach. "I have to tell you," he said in a serious voice. "There's no fighting allowed here. You'll be sent straight home if you get in a fight." He raised a finger. "It's a one-strike-and-you're-out policy." He paused and looked at Frederick, waiting for him to say something.

"Okay."

"Okay?" Benjamin said.

Frederick shrugged and nodded.

"Well, good then." Benjamin rolled onto the toes of his white tennis shoes and then dropped back on his heels. "Good for you, Dash."

The front doors of the main building opened and boys burst out of it, running for the food tent where Benjamin and Frederick waited.

"Oh!" Benjamin said. His face paled. "They're coming." The way he said it someone would've thought he was talking about *asteroids* coming to destroy all life on Earth, not some hungry campers coming to breakfast. He took a step back, putting Frederick between himself and the oncoming campers.

"May I get some more food?" Frederick asked, ignoring Benjamin's behavior.

"Sure!" Benjamin said. "Of course you can. Please help yourself."

"I mean . . . I just feel kind of bad because I already had some pancakes?" Frederick said, expecting Benjamin to retract his offer. After all, they probably had a limited amount of food for all the boys.

"Have all you want." Benjamin spread his hands wide as he backed away, toward the woods.

"Thanks!" Frederick said. "Thanks a lot!"

He hurried to be the first in the food line and got the plate off the top of the stack. As he was reaching for the tongs, he half turned to the boy who had just gotten in line behind him.

"Hi—" Frederick began, but before he could get another word out, the boy body-slammed him out of the line and sent him staggering into one of the folding chairs. Frederick clutched his plate to his chest like a shield.

Boys shouted and shoved. Stainless-steel lids clanged and clonged as they hit the table. The closest tent pole trembled like a tree in a storm. Boys brandished tongs that they snapped and clamped down on arms and noses. Then Frederick saw one of Miss Betty's beautiful golden pancakes fall to the ground.

A shoe stomped the pancake, and Frederick let out a strangled, "Hey!"

One of the boys closest to Frederick turned to look at him then. The boy was at the edge of the free-for-all, spinning a plate on one finger. When his eyes dropped to the name badge against Frederick's chest, the plate toppled. The boy lunged and caught it before it hit the ground. Then he looked up at Frederick again.

"You're Dash?" the boy asked in a tone of wonder. He was holding the plate in both hands now.

"Dash?" someone else said, turning to see who had spoken.

A hush fell among the boys closest to Frederick. While the rest of the campers carried on shouting and fighting, Frederick found himself in a pocket of calm. The boys stared at him, waiting for him to answer.

"*Uhh,*" said Frederick, touching his name badge. "Yeah . . . yes, I mean. I *am* Dashiell Blackwood."

Aargh. Why had he said *I* am *Dashiell Blackwood?* Nobody said *I* am *So-and-So.*

"I mean," Frederick said quickly, "*I'm* Dashiell Blackwood."

That sounded wrong, too.

"I'm Dashiell Blackwood." For some reason, Frederick said this in the deepest voice he could manage, like he was doing a Darth Vader impression.

"My friend Simon said you'd be here. He said y'all were here together last year," the plate spinner said. "I didn't even know you *could* come to Omigoshee twice." Then he took a step back and made a welcoming gesture. "Do you want to get in line in front of me?"

Frederick hesitated. He wasn't normally a line cutter. But then he remembered that he was at camp to make a fresh start and be more of a lion, and Fresh Start Frederick was exactly the kind of person who got asked to cut in line.

"Thanks," he said as he stepped in front of the other boy.

The boy bobbed his head. "Sure thing, Dash!"

The kids around them started talking again. Now that he was in line, Frederick realized that the deafening noise the boys were making was exciting, not frightening. Like a good pep rally.

"Which group are you in?" Frederick asked loudly over the clamor.

"Nine," the boy answered. He kept stealing glances at Frederick.

Frederick had been hoping they were in the same group. "I'm in Thirteen," he said. "But I bet we'll hang out with people from all the groups."

"Yeah." The boy nodded. "Sure, Dash."

When he reached the serving trays, Miss Betty's perfectly arranged pancakes were in disarray, smooshed and scattered. But Frederick picked out two that looked mostly untouched and put them on his plate. He got two more sausage links and a spoon-ful of breakfast potatoes. Then, before he headed off, he tried to think of something cool to say to his new friend.

"Well . . . ," he said. "I'll see you when I see you. I mean . . . I'll see you. Later."

The plate spinner blinked uncertainly. Frederick nodded and walked away.

He spent a long time at the condiment table, get-ting the exact right amount of syrup and layering butter pats onto his pancakes. He considered the strawberry jelly packets but decided the pancakes didn't need them.

By the time he made it to the table that had a sign with the number thirteen on it, four boys were already sitting there. Their cheeks were fat with pancakes. They clutched their forks in their fists and looked at Frederick with beady eyes. There were no empty chairs left at the table.

Frederick hovered for a moment, trying to figure out what he should do.

One of the campers at the table, a lean, stringy-looking boy with a buzz cut, swallowed and squinted at Frederick, his eyes darting down to the name tag and then back up to Frederick's face. His grip on his fork loosened, and his eyebrows rose.

"You're in our group, Dash?" he asked excitedly. Metal braces glinted on his teeth when he spoke.

The others' eyes widened. The boy with the braces didn't wait for Frederick to answer.

"Awesome!" he said. "Make some room for my man Dash." He waved his fork at a smaller boy who sat beside him.

The small boy didn't move. He tapped his plastic knife with one finger . . . *tap, tap, tap* . . . and glared at Frederick.

Frederick felt his shoulders hunching under the boy's stare. He started to say it was all right, he would find another chair and squeeze in, but then the boy with braces gave the glaring boy a shove. "Move it, Ant Bite," he said in a less friendly tone.

Ant Bite slapped the knife down. Then he sighed and stood, looping his arm around his plate and cup, scraping them sideways to clear a space for Frederick.

"*Umm*, thank you," Frederick said, and lowered himself into Ant Bite's seat.

Ant Bite stalked off to find another chair without looking back.

The others started eating again, shooting looks at Frederick every few seconds. He studied them as well.

The boy with the braces looked like he was Frederick's age.

The one sitting across from Frederick might have been their age, too, but he was huge. Everything about him was big. He was tall and wide. He had a big head and hands like shovels.

The third boy looked older and taller. He had a big chin with one of those chin dimples right in the middle, and as he ate, he was reading a book that lay spread open in his lap. Frederick glanced down at the boy's chest to read his name badge, but he wasn't wearing one.

None of them were wearing their lanyards. Frederick looked around and saw that none of the boys at the other tables were wearing lanyards either. He casually lifted his own over his head and dropped it on the ground beside his seat. Then he kicked it under the table.

The younger boy, Ant Bite, came back, dragging a chair.

"So," said Frederick. "Do you all go to the same school?" He wondered if they knew each other already. He hoped not. He didn't want it to be one of those situations where they had all these old stories and inside jokes and Frederick never knew what they were laughing about. He hated that.

"Nope," the big boy said around a mouthful of food. "I go to Pike County Middle."

Frederick had never heard of it. The boy with the braces shrugged at Frederick to show he'd never heard of it either, and then he shoved some potatoes in his mouth.

"I'm Nosebleed," the big boy who went to Pike County Middle added.

"Your name's *Nosebleed*?" Frederick said.

Nosebleed laughed—still with his mouth full so that Frederick saw wet gray chunks of pancake bouncing on his tongue. "No!" he said. "I'm *called* Nosebleed. That's my nickname."

Of course Frederick had known it was a nickname, because nobody's parents would actually write *Nosebleed* on a birth certificate, but he decided not to get into it.

"Why are you *called* Nosebleed?" he asked instead.

Nosebleed didn't answer. Instead, he lifted himself

off his chair and leaned sideways until he was over Ant Bite's plate. He pressed a finger against his nose, closing off one nostril.

"Hey!" Ant Bite said, trying to block Nosebleed with his arm.

But it was too late. Nosebleed . . . *blew*, and blood sprayed onto the potatoes and sausage.

Ant Bite yelled and shoved his plate away so hard that it slid off the other side of the table. Boys at the neighboring tables looked over at Group Thirteen in alarm.

"That's *nasty*, Nosebleed," said the boy with the braces, shaking his head. "What have we told you, man? Not while we're eating."

The older boy with the chin dimple was leaning back and holding his book over his shoulder, protecting it from the blood spray.

Frederick was frozen, staring.

"Do you have the *plague* or something?" he asked when he had found his voice.

Nosebleed laughed again. "No!" he said. "I have nosebleeds." He chuckled some more and sat down. He was still shaking with laughter as he stuffed a sausage in his mouth.

Frederick set his fork down.

"You don't want your pancakes?" Nosebleed asked.

"I'm not hungry anymore," Frederick said. "Forever," he added.

"I'm Specs," the boy with the braces said.

"Specs." Frederick's voice was wary.

"Like spectacles," Specs said in a hard voice. "Because whenever I see a pair of glasses, I get enraged and I have to snap 'em in twain."

"In twain," Frederick said. He could hear himself repeating Specs's words back to him like a parrot, but he couldn't help it. His brain was still processing the blood shower.

"In twain," Specs said again, and he slammed his fist on the table. "In two?" he said, raising his eyebrows at Frederick, like Frederick was being slow on the uptake, which he guessed he was.

"Why would anyone do that?" Frederick asked.

Specs leaned back in his chair, rearing it up on two legs. "My mom made me wear glasses when I was a little kid. And everybody picked on me. Until one day"—Specs brought the chair legs down with a *thud*—"I broke 'em in twain."

The boy who was reading sniffed and shook his head before he turned the page.

"Did you get in trouble?" Nosebleed asked Specs, his eyes wide, holding a pancake in either hand. "Because my cousin wears glasses, and they cost five hundred dollars."

Specs curled his lip, showing a glint of metal brackets. "Yeah." He shrugged. "I got in trouble. But I didn't care. And this guy at my school, Corbin Harris, saw me do it, and he said I was the wildest person he ever knew." The way Specs said this, it was clear that having Corbin Harris say you were the wildest person he knew was a high honor.

"So now," Specs said, "whenever I see somebody with glasses, I break 'em. It's just what I do. It's my *thing*."

"How can you see?" Nosebleed asked, leaning over the table so that he was closer to Specs. "Can you see me right now?"

"People who wear glasses can still see without them," Specs said.

"Do I look really blurry to you?" Nosebleed pressed.

"My friend Raj wears glasses," Frederick said. "He couldn't play baseball without them. He plays third base. He was on the all-star team last year."

"And if I met your buddy Raj, I'd break his glasses, too," Specs said, jutting out his chin.

Frederick thought that Specs had completely missed the point about how Raj's glasses were a good thing.

Nosebleed's mouth was full again as he pointed to the other two boys at the table. "We call *him* the Professor," he said, indicating the older boy with the chin dimple. The Professor glanced up from his book and nodded at Frederick. "And that's Ant Bite." Nosebleed gestured at the smaller boy beside Frederick, who was glaring at the empty table where his breakfast had been before it was bled on and slung to the ground.

Frederick guessed the Professor was the Professor because he liked to read, which was a lot more promising a nickname than "Specs" or "Nosebleed." But he wasn't sure why someone would be called *Ant Bite*. Did the kid *bite* people? Did he bite ants? Had he once had, like, a million ant bites and had to go to the hospital? Ant Bite didn't seem eager to discuss it.

"So what's *your* nickname?" Nosebleed asked.

"*Uhh,*" said Frederick, stalling for time. He'd never

had a nickname. Raj and Joel didn't have nicknames either.

These four boys had just met at the welcome meeting this morning, and they already all had nicknames, while Frederick—in his entire life—had never done anything to earn a nickname.

"Well," he said, thinking fast, "some people call me . . ." He paused, and then said the first name he thought of. "Frederick Frederickson."

The Professor looked up from his book, letting the cover fold closed. Ant Bite's permanent glare faltered and was replaced with a doubtful expression. Nosebleed and Specs blinked at each other, and then they burst into laughter.

"That's the dumbest nickname I ever heard of," the Professor said, awed, over the sound of their guffaws.

For some reason, that made the other two laugh even harder.

"Yeah, how'd you even come up with a name that dumb?" Specs asked as he gasped for air. "Frederick Frederickson." Specs shook his head and slapped Frederick's back so hard that Frederick jerked forward, his face nearly hitting his breakfast.

Frederick smiled weakly and shrugged.

"You're the funniest guy I ever met." Nosebleed was wiping his eyes.

Frederick looked around. He realized he was waiting for someone to disagree and say he wasn't that funny, but no one did. All the others were smiling, too. Even Ant Bite smiled a little. Though he was still holding his knife in his fist.

No one had ever told Frederick he was funny. And even though the thing they were laughing at was his own name, he found that it felt good to make people laugh. It made him feel happy . . . popular . . . powerful. He picked up his fork and started digging into his food. The breakfast potatoes were peppery and crispy on the outside.

"I wondered where you were when I saw your name on the registration," Specs said. "My brother's told me all about you. He goes to the Straker Academy. You got sent there, too, right? Before you were kicked out? Anyway, you weren't on the bus, so how'd you get here?"

Frederick paused with his fork halfway to his mouth, brain reeling, wondering what the Straker Academy was and what Specs's brother had said

about Dashiell. If anyone at camp *knew* Dashiell—
the real Dashiell—then they would know that
Frederick wasn't him.

"Yeah," said Nosebleed, "how'd you get here?"

"Umm . . . I . . ." Frederick stammered. His mind
was a blank empty hole of nothingness and . . . and
more nothingness. "I stole a boat and came down on
the river."

Everyone at the table went still and looked at
Frederick, and Frederick gulped down the pancake
he was eating, realizing what he'd just said and how
it sounded. Dangerous, illegal.

"Did you really steal a boat?" Ant Bite was looking
Frederick in the eye.

"*Uhh* . . . ," Frederick said. Were they going to tell
on him? He needed to explain that he'd been joking.
Or, at least, that it wasn't the way it sounded. "Well—"

"That's classic Dash," Specs said, shaking his head
in appreciation.

Nosebleed was gazing at Frederick, a forgotten
sausage in his hand.

The Professor was smiling to himself, his eyes far
away, like he was imagining what it must be like to
commandeer a boat and navigate it down a dark river.

"*Huh*," Ant Bite said, tilting his head back. He set his knife down.

Frederick shifted in his seat. He was pleased that the boys seemed to be so impressed with him, but he didn't know if he should let them think he stole stuff all the time.

"You can't fight while you're here, though," Specs said. "They're serious about that."

Frederick made an annoyed sound. "Why does everyone keep saying that? I'm not going to get in a fight."

"Is that what you said before your face got like that?" the Professor asked, pointing his book at Frederick.

"Oh!" Frederick said, his hand going up to his broken nose. "This? This wasn't a fight."

"That's right," Specs said, slapping the table and grinning. "'Twas but a light skirmish for our man Dash."

"You've got blood on your shirt," Nosebleed said. "Cold water'll get that out."

Frederick looked down at the T-shirt he'd been wearing since yesterday. It was spattered with dark specks.

"He got you good," the Professor observed, eyeing Frederick's nose.

"Hey," Specs said. "Don't be disrespectful. I bet Dash got the other guy good, too."

"What *did* the other guy look like when you were done with him?" Nosebleed said eagerly, leaning forward and gazing at Frederick as he took a bite of sausage.

"Well," Frederick said, considering. "He's about my height. He has reddish hair."

Ant Bite groaned and covered his eyes with his hands.

Nosebleed laughed so hard that chewed sausage spewed out of his mouth and onto the table.

"So," Specs said, leaning in toward Frederick, squeezing his fork in his fist. "Is it true what they say about you?" he asked in a low voice.

Nosebleed, the Professor, and Ant Bite went still, and Frederick knew they were hanging on every word.

"Is—is what true?" Frederick asked.

"What you did with the iguana and the Cabbage Patch Kid," Specs said eagerly. "Is it true?"

Frederick looked around at the other boys and

shifted in his seat. It probably wasn't right, taking credit for something he hadn't done. But then he saw Specs lick his lips. Ant Bite was listening. The Professor had forgotten his book, and Nosebleed was ignoring his food. Frederick remembered that powerful feeling he'd had when he'd made them laugh, and now he wanted to see their faces light up again and know that he was the one responsible for that excitement.

"It's the whole truth," he said in a low voice. "And nothing *but* the truth." He swallowed and crossed his fingers beneath the table. "So help me God."

There was a moment of silence at the table, everyone holding their breath.

Then one word escaped Nosebleed, like a sigh. "Wow."

7

For Whom the Bell Tolls

FOR THE FIRST TIME IN HIS LIFE, FREDERICK WAS popular. The boys in his group were eager to tell him stories and rumors about the other campers. Specs waited to see if Frederick laughed at a joke before he would laugh himself. The Professor put his book down so that he could listen to Frederick talk about his night on the river. Nosebleed kept trying to get his attention.

Only Ant Bite didn't seem to be completely impressed by Dashiell Blackwood, but Frederick didn't need him when he had three other admirers.

Frederick had always thought that being popular and having all the other kids want to sit by him and talk to him would be a great feeling . . . and he'd been absolutely right. It was the *greatest* feeling in the entire world. Frederick was warm and full of pancakes and confidence. If Benjamin had announced that there was a ticking bomb under one of the tables, Frederick would've been able to dismantle it, because of the power of his confidence. He wondered if this was what Devin Goodyear felt like all the time.

After breakfast, the groups split up and went off to different activities. The boys in Groups Nine through Thirteen followed their counselors around the main building and stopped beneath a lumber frame that was, according to Benjamin, twelve feet tall. White sandbags were thrown over the legs of the frame, and five evenly spaced ropes hung down from the beam at the top. Thick knots were tied at intervals along the length of each rope, and high up, at the top of every rope, hung a metal bell with a short pull. One rope and one bell for each group.

Group Ten's counselor, whose name was Eric, stepped beside one of the ropes and spun around to face the assembled boys and counselors. He planted his feet wide and blew a shrill whistle.

Eric was a sports management major from

Piedmont State. He wore the same blue polo and khaki shorts that all the counselors wore, but while Benjamin's shorts would have fit a Transformer, Eric's were sized for a Ken doll. He had tall white socks that stretched to his kneecaps, and he wore sunglasses so reflective the lenses looked like molten silver. In addition to being Ten's counselor, he was also the head counselor for the entire camp.

Eric clicked the trigger on a battery-powered megaphone. "Listen up, maggots!" his voice growled mechanically through the megaphone. "This is a relay. That means TEAMWORK, maggots! Each group will send one man at a time up the rope." He gave the rope closest to him a tug, just in case they weren't sure what a rope was. "When you get to the top, you ring the bell. Then you come back down, and the next one of you goes up.

"If you don't ring the bell," Eric continued, "it doesn't count. The first team to have all five people ring the bell . . . *wins*." The last word reverberated through the trees.

Frederick stepped over to Benjamin. "What do we win?" he asked in a low voice.

Benjamin blinked at him.

"What do we win?" Frederick repeated. He was thinking they might earn points or get candy, or perhaps they would have the privilege of keeping possession of a special trophy until some other group won it away from them. Frederick hoped that he would be the one who got to carry the trophy around.

"Oh," Benjamin said brightly, understanding. "I'll find out." He waved his hand. "Eric!" he called, interrupting Eric's instructions about when the relay would begin and what various blasts on his whistle meant. "Eric!"

The sun flashed off Eric's silver lenses, reflecting blue skies and puffy white clouds. Everyone turned to look at Benjamin and Group Thirteen. Frederick sidestepped behind his counselor.

"What do the boys win if they're the first team to finish?" Benjamin asked.

There was a moment of silence. The campers looked from Benjamin to Eric.

"The boys who win . . . ," Eric said slowly, *"win."* And the way he said the word *win*, like he was squeezing the life out of it, made it sound like winning was the most primal and satisfying thing a person could do.

"Oh," said Benjamin, and he turned around to look at Frederick. "You don't get anything if you win," he said, sounding disappointed.

But Frederick realized that Eric was right. He didn't need a trophy or a prize. Winning—winning something for his team—his teammates looking at him with happiness and awe . . . that was the only thing in the world that Frederick wanted.

"You have sixty seconds," Eric said into his megaphone. "And then on my whistle . . ."

Immediately all the boys started talking, forming tight clusters around their counselors. Frederick turned to his group, eager to discuss their plan. He was about to ask the other guys if they had any ideas, but Nosebleed was already talking.

"Are you going to break *his* glasses?" Nosebleed jerked his head at Eric.

"Those are *sun*glasses," Specs said.

"So you can see that they're sunglasses all the way from here?" Nosebleed asked.

"Who's going first?" Frederick asked, wanting to get them on track so they'd have time to make a plan.

Frederick was a little nervous about the whole situation. He definitely wanted to do the relay and win, but he had never climbed a rope before. He was sure that he *could* climb it; he just wished he could do a practice run in private.

None of the others seemed anxious. Nosebleed and Specs weren't even paying attention to the rope. The Professor was gazing up at Group Thirteen's bell with a grim but resigned expression. Ant Bite was standing apart from the group and kicking rocks at Group Eleven.

At this rate, they were going to be the only ones who weren't ready when Eric blew his whistle.

"Hey," Frederick said, trying to talk over Nosebleed and Specs's bickering. "Come on. We need a plan."

"Okay," Benjamin said, squeezing into the loose circle the boys had formed. "What order are you guys climbing in?"

"It's a relay. It doesn't matter who goes first," the Professor said, bending his paperback in his hands.

"This matters," Frederick said in annoyance. The Professor sounded like he didn't care.

"No, no," Specs said eagerly, turning away from Nosebleed and finally focusing on the matter at hand. He lowered his voice so the other groups wouldn't overhear him. "We put our best climbers first and strike icy fear into the hearts of our enemies."

Ant Bite still hadn't joined the group. He was frowning at a rock on the ground, then at a boy from Group Eleven. His face was scrunched in concentration, like he was calculating the trajectory between rock and boy.

"Okay, who are our best climbers?" Nosebleed asked, drawing himself up and looking at each of the other boys as if he was expecting one of them to say, *Well, I'm the third-ranked rope climber of all boys, aged ten to twelve, in the Southeast.*

No one said that. It would've been surprising if anyone had.

"You could go in alphabetical order," Benjamin suggested. "Or you could go in order from oldest to youngest. Or youngest to oldest."

Nosebleed dabbed his nose and checked his fingertips to see if there was any blood. "Dash, do you want to go first?" he asked.

Panic punched Frederick in the chest.

The others looked at him, waiting for him to answer. He made a noncommittal noise in his throat and shrugged, spreading his hands open in a vague gesture that might have meant *No, I don't want to climb the rope first*, but it equally could've meant *Yes, I would love another canapé.*

"What's this mean?" The Professor wrinkled his forehead and mimicked Frederick's shrug. "What's that mean?" he asked the others.

Nosebleed shrugged back at him.

The group next to them had finished their planning and formed a line and was doing a synchronized battle chant that involved clapping and stomping.

"I know!" said Benjamin. "We could find out what month your birthdays are and do it in order of whose birthday's soonest. That's a good idea. When's your birthday, Ant Bite?"

They all turned to look at Ant Bite just as the younger boy swung his foot and sent a rock stinging into a boy's calf. The kid yelped and spun around to glare at them.

"*Ant Bite*," Benjamin said in a shocked voice. "We don't kick rocks at people."

"I'll go first," the Professor said, shaking his head. He set his book on the ground, looked at the rope again, and took a deep breath.

"Okay," Frederick said, the tension in his chest easing. "Who's going to—"

Then Eric's whistle sounded, and boys from the other groups ran to their ropes. The Professor turned to the others, spreading his hands like he was waiting on a decision.

"Go!" Frederick yelled.

The Professor strode over to the rope, gave a jump, and grabbed on. Then he started to climb. He didn't make it look easy, but he moved, hand over hand, up the rope at about the same speed as the boys from the other four groups, the whole time wearing the same grim, kill-or-be-killed expression.

On the ground, the boys called up useful advice that the climbers might not have thought of by themselves.

"Use your arms!"

"Use your legs!"

"Climb faster!"

"You need to be higher!"

Frederick found himself clapping his hands together like a seal and barking, "Climb faster! Climb higher! Use your legs!" because even though he had never climbed a rope before, he suddenly knew—as if the knowledge of how to climb a rope had been passed down from his vine-climbing ancestors and had been waiting in his cells to be activated at this very moment—that these were helpful and good things to shout at someone who was climbing a rope.

"Climb higher!" he yelled, and he was sure it was his shouts that encouraged the Professor upward.

The Professor was the second boy to ring a bell. Clinging to the rope tightly with one hand and his legs, he reached out and gave the bell a good pull, making a clanging sound that had to satisfy even Eric of the Teeny Shorts.

Then he climbed back down the rope, sliding the last few inches.

"Go!" Frederick said, giving Specs a shove in the shoulder before the other boy could suggest that Frederick go next.

Specs didn't climb as fast as the Professor. He wasted a lot of time trying and failing to wrap the rope around his legs. His legs flailed so much that Frederick and Nosebleed started yelling, *"Don't* use your legs! *Don't* use your legs!"

By the time Specs finally rang the bell, Group Ten

and Group Eleven had already sent their third boys up. Group Nine was struggling.

On the ground, Frederick was gripping handfuls of his hair and jumping up and down. Specs was just as slow coming down as he had been going up. When he finally made it back to the earth, Frederick spun around to see who was next and found Ant Bite looking right at him.

Frederick froze, sure that the other boy could see the fear that must be flashing out of his eyes like Morse code. Was Ant Bite going to tell everyone that Frederick was scared? But he just shook his head at Frederick. Then he ran for the rope and started up it.

Frederick sagged with relief. He needed a little more time to prepare. He needed to limber up and figure out how he was going to climb the rope and still look cool. There must be a special way cool people did things that made them look cool. *How would Dash climb the rope?* Frederick asked himself.

"Oh my gosh," Benjamin said. "Look at him go."

"He's like Tarzan," Nosebleed said. "Only angry. And he's wearing a shirt . . . and shoes."

Their talking distracted Frederick from his thoughts. He looked up.

Ant Bite was moving twice as fast as anyone else. His hands snatched at the rope. His face angled upward, and he glared at the bell, looking like once he got to the top he was going to murder it.

"Whoa," Frederick muttered.

All the other campers on the ground were gazing at Group Thirteen's rope, too. Even Eric was watching Ant Bite, the small boy reflected twice in his sunglasses as he rang the bell at the top.

Ant Bite skimmed down the rope so fast that Group Thirteen was level with Group Ten again. They were still in this thing.

Frantic, Frederick turned to Nosebleed, and he was opening his mouth to encourage the other boy and yell at him to "Climb! Climb higher!" but Nosebleed reached out and pushed Frederick toward the rope just as Ant Bite ran up and tagged his arm, signaling it was his turn to climb. Frederick knew that the moment had come. He couldn't put it off any longer.

He jogged over.

The rope was rough and prickly, almost splintery. Its tiny bristles pricked Frederick's palms, but he clung to it, picking his feet up. He put one hand higher up, grabbed a knot, and with a mighty effort, hoisted himself. He looked up the rope and saw the bell, a speck in the distance, outlined by blazing blue sky. He looked back down the rope. The bottoms of his tennis shoes were six inches off the ground. "Oh, shoot."

"Come on, Dash!" Nosebleed yelled. "Climb higher!"

Frederick growled through his teeth as his arms shook. *Obviously* he needed to climb higher. Did they think he was stupid? Did they think he had somehow forgotten why he was on the rope?

"Use your legs!" the Professor called.

Frederick was *trying* to use his legs. Didn't they see him trying?

He pulled himself six inches higher. Sweat oozed out of his hands. This was impossible. But Frederick couldn't let his team down. The Professor had climbed. Specs had climbed. And Ant Bite. He had to get to the top of the rope, to reach out and grab the bell pull. Frederick let go with one hand and grabbed higher. He hauled himself up. He tried to put his feet against a knot, but the rope snaked out from between his shoes, slithering away from him. *Why*, Frederick wondered, *did everything have to be so hard? Why couldn't something be easy, just once?*

Somehow, Frederick slowly made his way up the rope. He heard the bells ringing all around him. He heard the campers shouting. Then he heard cheering, and he knew that some other group had gotten all their boys to the top, and Group Thirteen wasn't going to win. But still Frederick climbed. He wasn't going to quit. He wasn't going to go back down that rope and see his team's disappointed faces. Not without ringing that bell first. It would be okay if he could just ring the bell.

Then Frederick had made it. He reached out with one burning, spaghetti-noodle arm and grabbed the short rope beneath the bell and gave a sharp tug. The bell sounded—*clang-a-lang*—and for one glorious moment it was as though Frederick's heart was *clang-a-lang*ing back. He'd done it!

But then his arm—the arm that was hanging on to the splintery climbing rope—cramped, went limp, and let go. Frederick now swung from the bell, clutching the pull with only one hand.

He screamed and grabbed with the other flailing

hand, catching the bell's short rope and squeezing it for dear life.

Frederick's arms were straight. He was hanging from the bell like a giant, Frederick-shaped bell pull. His legs kicked out, scrambling for purchase. There was nothing but air.

Beneath him the other campers were shouting—he couldn't hear what they shouted because his ears weren't working properly. His brain wasn't working properly either, because Frederick had two thoughts as he hung there.

And they weren't helpful thoughts, like how to grab the other rope or ideas for how to save himself. No, the first was *I really hate this*, and by *this* he meant the entire situation. He hated ropes and he hated bells and he hated that guys named Eric with tall socks and short shorts scared him. His second thought as he swung there was actually a vision—a vision of Raj and Joel shaking their heads. *Let's look at the facts*, Joel had said.

Then the short rope slipped out of his hands, and he hurtled toward the ground.

8

Ding-a-Ling

FREDERICK WAS ON HIS BACK, HIS EYES SQUEEZED shut. His hands burned. His arms ached. His heart, which had just been clang-a-langing like a bell, was now thunk-a-lunking like a peg-legged pirate tumbling down a flight of stairs.

Through his haze of panic and pain, Frederick became aware of a heaviness filling his chest, threatening to overflow like a dam. His eyes stung, and he realized with horror that he was about to cry.

His eyelids snapped open. Nosebleed, Specs, the Professor, Ant Bite, and Benjamin were all leaning over him, blocking out the sky. When they saw he was conscious, they let out their breath.

"We thought you were dead!" Nosebleed said.

"Don't move a muscle—" Benjamin began.

Frederick ignored them and scrambled to his feet. He pushed between Benjamin and Nosebleed and started walking as fast as he could through the groups of campers and around the climbing frame. He walked this way and then changed direction and walked that way.

Frederick was power walking, his arms pumping like pistons and his legs speedboating him around and around the yard. He wove in and out between the other boys, aware of them giving him strange looks and jumping out of the way so he wouldn't brush against them. Frederick knew he looked stupid, but he didn't care, because as long as he kept moving the tears wouldn't catch up.

"Zero nine hundred hours!" Eric shouted into his megaphone as he strode through the boys. "Swimming rotation! I want you changed and riverside in five!" He dodged out of the way as Frederick sped by him. "Quit playing around, Dash!" he said. Then he gave two short blasts on his whistle.

The boys broke up, heading toward their cabins, several of them leaping sideways as Frederick motored past them.

He made it back to Group Thirteen, where the boys and Benjamin were waiting for him. Frederick stopped in the middle of the group, leaning over and putting his hands on his knees. The heavy, about-to-spill-over feeling in his chest had eased. He had outrun the tears.

"Okay," Frederick said, and let out a whoosh of air through his mouth. "Okay. I'm all right."

"That was . . ." Benjamin trailed off and shook his head. "That was the . . . *weirdest* thing I've ever seen."

"You looked like you had *bees* chasing you," Nosebleed said.

"Why'd you try to hang on to the bell?" Specs asked.

"He didn't *mean* to hang on to the bell," the Professor said to Specs. "He accidentally let go of the rope."

"Well, why'd he let go of the rope?" Specs demanded.

"*Ac-ci-dent*," Ant Bite sounded out each syllable loudly for Specs.

Specs shoved the younger boy's arm.

Then Frederick turned to Nosebleed and said, "Your turn."

"*My* turn?" Nosebleed put his hands on his chest as if to say, *Who, me?*

Frederick's own chest heaved. "You have to climb." He pointed at the rope, but his arm felt like it weighed three hundred pounds, and it flopped back to his side.

"The race is over," the Professor said.

Frederick shook his head. "That doesn't matter." He could hear that what he was saying sounded unreasonable, but he couldn't seem to do anything about it. The words were falling out of his mouth without his having any control over them. He gestured clumsily at Nosebleed. "He has to climb."

"The Professor's right, Dash," Benjamin said. "We should go get changed. Don't you want to go swimming?"

"I can't climb," Nosebleed said to Frederick.

"What?" Frederick said, panting.

"I. Can't. Climb." Nosebleed said each word loudly and slowly. He pointed with both hands at his nose. "If I exert myself, my nose will bleed."

"What? If you *exert* yourself?" Frederick looked at the others. "Did you hear that?" he demanded. "He can't even climb. He can't even climb because he would *exert* himself."

"Whatever, man, it's over," the Professor said in a just-drop-it tone. He bent down and scooped up his book.

"We didn't win," Frederick said, his voice cracking. He was getting shrill, and he knew that wasn't cool, but he couldn't let it go.

"And whose fault is that?" Specs asked, accusation in his voice.

"Sometimes you win," Benjamin said. "And sometimes you lose, but either way you *learn*."

"We didn't *lose*, either," Frederick said. "We didn't even *finish*."

"I think not finishing qualifies as losing," the Professor pointed out.

"I know this is disheartening," Benjamin said. His hands fluttered, adjusting his name badge.

Frederick didn't feel disheartened. He felt like he was an incredibly tiny person, like the size of a flea, and a larger, evil person was holding a magnifying glass over him, directing a beam of sunlight to try and burn him up, and Frederick was shouting for help but no one could understand him because he had a tiny little flea voice.

"You were never even going to climb!" Frederick said to Nosebleed. "And you!" He walked up to Specs and got in his face. The other boy stuck out his chin and didn't budge.

"You didn't really hold up a bank with a hand grenade and a parasol, did you?" Specs asked with narrowed eyes, studying Frederick like he was seeing him clearly for the first time.

"You were . . . so . . . slow," Frederick said. "You were slower than a—a . . ."

"Sloth?" the Professor suggested.

"Sloths live in trees," Ant Bite said.

The Professor looked in surprise at Ant Bite and then said, "Oh, yeah."

"So what?" Frederick yelled, turning on Ant Bite and looming over him menacingly.

Ant Bite didn't look menaced. "So animals that live in trees are probably good climbers." The smaller boy shrugged.

"That's . . . that's a really good point," Frederick said. His voice faltered and died, and he stared at a spot on the ground because he couldn't seem to meet anyone's eyes.

It was important to Frederick that everyone in Group Thirteen and everyone in every other group and every human being on the planet understand that *he* was not the one who had let his team down. Yes, he was part of it. But it wasn't just him! Nosebleed couldn't climb at all; he wasn't even going to try. And Specs had lost them valuable time; if he had done better, they might not have gotten so far behind. But no one was going to remember that, because Frederick had gone last and because he had fallen from the bell.

"Hey," Specs said with a pleased note in his voice.

Frederick dragged his gaze up to look at the other boy, and something in the way one half of Specs's mouth curled up in a smile gave Frederick a bad feeling—no, a bad *certainty*—about what was coming next.

"I've thought of a nickname for you," Specs said, squinting at Frederick. "We can call you Ding-a-Ling."

Frederick swallowed and looked at the ground again. None of the others said anything.

"The way you were swinging from that bell," Specs went on, and he let out a short, fake laugh. "It was hilarious. *Ding, ding, ding.* You looked like something out of a cartoon."

"Wait a second, Specs," Benjamin began.

"Cut it out," the Professor said to Specs.

Specs spread his hands wide in a gesture of innocence and then turned on his heel and sauntered after the other groups.

"I think . . . ," Frederick said, more to himself than anyone else. "I think I'm ready to go home." Not that home would be any better; home was terrible, too. But at least at home there were no ropes to climb and no teammates to let down. The fact that he'd thought this camp would be his Big Opportunity seemed ridiculous to him now, and he was mad at himself for being so stupid.

"You know you can't go home, Dash," Benjamin said in a gentle voice. "You have to stay the whole weekend so that you can finish the program and be transformed."

"What?" said Frederick. He looked up. Nosebleed was shuffling his feet and watching Specs, who was heading for the sleeping cabins. The Professor had crossed his arms and was tapping the dimple in his chin with one finger. Ant Bite stood apart from the group.

"What program?" Frederick asked. "Transformed into what?" *Transformed.* That sounded like something butterflies did. Or Autobots. Or people on plastic surgery reality shows.

"Well," Benjamin said. "You know . . . Transformed into a person who's . . . Transformed into a better . . . *uhh* . . ."

"What kind of camp is this?" Frederick asked, a fresh wave of alarm building in him.

"Oh, it's a great camp!" Benjamin said. "It's a place to have fun and—"

"It's a disciplinary camp," Ant Bite said, interrupting Benjamin.

"*Disciplinary* camp?" Frederick repeated.

"It's a place to have *fun!*" Benjamin stressed. "And be transformed at the same time!"

"That's not . . ." Frederick's voice trailed off. *Disciplinary?* That was, like, for punishing kids, wasn't it? Why were they at a camp for punishing kids?

He looked, then, at Nosebleed, appreciating how very large the boy was. Not just heavy but strong, strong enough to slam Frederick to the ground. And the Professor, he wasn't a little guy. And Ant Bite, the way his eyes were sizing Frederick up. The way he had kicked those rocks at the others. *Snap 'em in twain,* Specs's voice echoed in Frederick's head. The boys in Groups One through Five were loping up to the ropes for their turn at the climbing relay. They whooped and swung from them, making the climbing frame sway dangerously.

These were *bad* kids, Frederick realized. Not like regular bad kids who didn't make their beds or eat their vegetables. These boys were bad like Lex Luthor or Magneto or Cruella de Vil, only not her because she was a lady, so that was a bad example.

"Oh," Frederick said.

"Do you have a problem with that?" Ant Bite asked.

"Wha— *No,*" Frederick said. "I don't have a problem. I'm *fine.* I think disciplinary camps are great. And the people who go to them are great. Just . . . great." He answered instinctively, not wanting to offend them.

"You had to know it was a disciplinary camp," the Professor said. "It was on the application."

"There was an application?" Nosebleed asked, looking around. "I didn't know there was an application."

"We need to get changed," Ant Bite said, turning his eyes away from Frederick, "if we're going swimming."

He took off after Specs. The others turned, too. Even Benjamin started to head away.

"Come on, Dash," Benjamin cajoled, like he was trying to get a scared puppy to follow him. "Let's go swimming, okay?"

9

The Dead Zone

NONE OF THE COUNSELORS OR OTHER CAMPERS seemed to find it odd that Dashiell had arrived at a transformational-slash-disciplinary camp for a three-day weekend without any swim trunks for taking a dip in the river. Or pajamas for sleeping in, or a change of clothes, an extra pair of shoes, sunscreen, a toothbrush . . . his own pillow from home.

While the other boys went into the sleeping cabins to change into their trunks, Frederick stayed outside and repeated to Benjamin that he didn't have anything to swim in, so what was he supposed to do while everyone else was in the river?

Benjamin frowned at Eric, who was barking orders

through the door of Group Ten's cabin. And then he frowned in the direction of the school bus, which was rolling out of the parking lot. Finally, he frowned at Frederick standing before him with his enormous nose and the wrinkled and bloodstained clothes that he'd worn to school the day before.

"You can swim in the shorts you're wearing?" Benjamin said, his tone making the sentence a question. "And they'll dry out?" A smile lit his face. "And then they'll be clean!"

"*Uhh*," said Frederick.

"Two birds," Benjamin said, lifting a finger philosophically, "one stone."

"What about my toothbrush?" Frederick said. He thought that this detail would for sure make Benjamin reconsider the conversation. "I can't brush my teeth without a toothbrush."

"I don't think you'll get cavities from not brushing your teeth for a few nights," Benjamin said.

"Are you a dentist?" Frederick demanded.

Benjamin blinked at him. Frederick looked around, and when he saw that no one was within earshot, he took a step closer to Benjamin, held the counselor's eyes, and explained rapidly.

"Listen, I really don't belong here. I'm Frederick Frederickson. I'm not Dashiell Whoever. And I accidentally stole my friend's dad's boat and the motor just fell off in the water, and I was going to swim back but there was this alligator, and I had to defend myself with a hamburger." He paused to suck in a big breath of air. "I need to get home," he finished.

He expected Benjamin to look surprised and then for realization to dawn on his face. And then the counselor would lead him away to some safe, air-conditioned room where he would wait for his parents to come and collect him.

But the look of surprise never came. What happened instead was that Benjamin took a breath and focused on a spot over Frederick's head for a moment. Then he looked back at Frederick with the closest thing to determination Frederick had ever seen on the counselor's face.

"I'm going to tell you a secret, Dash," Benjamin said. His voice was serious, like he had come to a big decision.

Frederick didn't want to hear Benjamin's big secret. He wanted to go home! But he thought it might sound rude if he told Benjamin that, so he swallowed the yell of frustration that was trying to get out.

"Okay," Frederick said in a tight voice, hoping that *after* the big secret thing, they would focus on the real problem.

"Okay," Benjamin said. "So we had to interview to be counselors. There was this whole long process where we got training and then took tests. It was really competitive. Everybody wants to be a counselor because it looks good on your résumé . . ."

Frederick's eyes wandered over the camp as Benjamin spoke. Two boys were sneaking behind the main cabin, cans of spray paint in their hands.

"I really, really wanted them to pick me to be a counselor," Benjamin said.

"*Uh-huh,*" Frederick said, trying to hurry him through the story. "And they did. They picked you."

"But when I got my official letter," Benjamin said, "I was rejected."

"What?" Frederick looked back at Benjamin. "But . . . you're here . . ."

Benjamin nodded. "They rejected my application," he said. "And I was really down about it." He took a breath and then smiled. "But then one of the counselors that got accepted got strep throat, and the camp called me to come in at the last minute." He bounced on the balls of his feet. "And I was nervous at first. I'm still nervous. But I believe that I can do this. I belong here. Even if I don't feel like it sometimes. I. Belong."

He reached out and put a hand on Frederick's shoulder. "And I believe that you belong here, too."

"I'm not Dash," Frederick said loudly. "I'm Frederick Frederickson!"

"You don't want to be here because you're afraid that the program won't work for you. That's a normal reaction for someone who's in the fear stage of the transformational process," Benjamin said in a voice that had the bossy yet soothing tone of a training manual.

"It's not a reaction!" Frederick said. "It's the truth."

"Once that fear has run its course, you'll be ready to transform." Benjamin's eyes were shining with hope. "The Camp Omigoshee program is going to work for you." He patted Frederick's shoulder. "You think about what I said. You *belong*."

The boys stood on the riverbank while Eric yelled into his megaphone about the dangers of the water.

All the boys were in swim trunks except for Ant Bite, who was in swim trunks and a reflective orange life vest, and Frederick, who was in his shorts. They waved away gnats as Eric's evil robot voice carried over the river and through the trees, punctuated by the distant sound of the climbing bells' clanging.

These were some of the dangers Eric covered in his speech: currents that could sweep them away in a moment; sharp objects on the river bottom that might puncture their bare feet and cause infections and lead to amputation of the affected limb; roughhousing and horseplay, which might cause drowning and dying; swimming under the water and then coming up under a log and knocking themselves unconscious, which, again, might result in a nasty case of death.

Eric didn't tell them how to *avoid* any of these outcomes, he just let them know that there was a very real possibility these things might happen. When he was done, Frederick raised his hand.

Eric's sunglasses pointed at him for a long moment before the counselor clicked the megaphone's trigger. "What is it, Dash?"

"What about alligators?" Frederick asked.

"What about them?" Eric said.

Frederick looked around at the others. They were kicking the sand like bulls pawing the ground.

"How do we . . ." Frederick tried to think of the right way to frame what he really wanted to know, which was *How can we get some sonar equipment in here and make sure that the river's clear? How can we make sure that we don't get eaten? How can we ever live without fear again?* "How can we know if there are alligators?"

Click went the megaphone. "You can't," Eric said. "Any more questions?"

Frederick gulped.

Eric turned his face skyward for a moment, as if asking the universe how he was supposed to endure the existence of boys like Frederick. When he looked back down, he clicked the megaphone. "Men of character don't obsess over what could go wrong, Dash. They're aware of the dangers and proceed anyway."

Frederick thought that he was never going to be a man of character, and also that maybe Eric was suggesting something illegal.

"Everyone in the water!" Eric ordered.

The boys raced to the water. They hit the river with giant splashes, crashing into it and pushing forward as if they were diving into beautiful, clear, safe water instead of murky, tea-colored water concealing a multitude of potentially lethal dangers.

Ant Bite followed more slowly. He walked into the river, holding on to the straps of his life vest. The younger boy eased out until he was bobbing like a cork. A glowering cork. The current spun him around and carried him down the river as the other boys splashed.

Frederick crept to the river's edge. Water lapped the tips of his big toes. The cool water *did* feel good. He thought maybe he could just wade a little bit, up to the shins. He was sure that he would be able to see an alligator coming if he was in the shallow water. Or the alligator would eat one of the boys farther out. He sensed someone behind him and turned to find Eric's sunglasses looking down at him.

"Get in the water, Dash," the counselor said. It was the first time Frederick had heard Eric's voice without the megaphone, and for some reason that made it super creepy. His lips didn't seem to move enough when he spoke. "You have ten seconds."

Frederick thought about trying to explain his situation to Eric. But he suspected that the head counselor wasn't going to be understanding or sympathetic. And he'd probably say Frederick was just at the fear stage of the transformational process.

Frederick waded out into the river up to his knees and then stepped off into the deep. The river was cold, and being in its dark water felt familiar. When Frederick closed his eyes, he could almost imagine that it was just like the times his dad had taken him to the public section of the Omigoshee back home.

When he opened his eyes, he could imagine the same thing. The other boys were swimming and splashing. Two were racing for the opposite bank. To someone who didn't know any better, they were acting just like regular boys.

But Frederick knew that they were acting that way because they thought they were all equals. If they knew that they had a law-abiding citizen in their midst, they'd probably attack. It was like how if you had a school of sharks sharking around in the ocean, they would just peacefully swim around in circles, but if you threw in a flounder—WHAM!—they would surge into a feeding frenzy, slashing with their teeth and tearing the flounder to pieces, leaving a murk of blood in the water.

Frederick was the flounder in this scenario. He was a flea on the butt of a meerkat and a ding-a-ling and a flounder. He wasn't feeling sorry for himself. He was just being realistic. And now that he was being realistic, Frederick admitted to himself that he just wanted to get away from here and get back home where he was safe.

Frederick paddled over to where Nosebleed was floating.

The other boy's face and feet bobbed above the surface of the water. Everything in between sank.

"Hey," Frederick said. "Do you think I could borrow your phone when we get back to the cabin?"

Nosebleed didn't open his eyes, and Frederick thought maybe he'd fallen asleep and hadn't heard, but then he said in a lazy voice, "Sure thing, Dash."

"Really?" Frederick asked in surprise. "That's great." He hadn't expected it to be that easy. He would just use Nosebleed's phone to call his mom, and she would drive like a NASCAR racer to pick him up.

"Of course," Nosebleed said, opening his eyes and rolling over in the water, "you can't make a *call* with it."

"What?" Frederick's vision of his mother speeding toward him vanished.

"There's no service out here. You can't make a phone call."

"There's a little bit of service," Frederick argued.

"Nope," said Nosebleed.

"Yes," Frederick insisted. "There's always a little bit of service. There can't be *none*." It wasn't possible that there was a place where you couldn't make a phone call. Because this was America and the twenty-first century, and things like that didn't happen anymore.

Frederick swam over to the Professor. "Hey," he said. "Is it true you can't use a cell phone here?"

"Yeah," the Professor said, and he started swimming away from Frederick.

Frederick kicked after him, his need for answers greater than his fear of alligators. "Like you *can't* can't?" Frederick called after him, spitting out a mouthful of water. "Not just that it's against the rules?"

"Listen," the Professor said. "I'm swimming by myself right now, okay?"

Frederick's arms churned the surface of the water. "Okay," he said. "Sure."

A few of the boys swimming nearby had overheard, and they were looking over at Frederick with bright, interested eyes.

"Who are you going to call, Dash?" one boy asked.

"Someone on the outside?" a voice suggested.

"Are you sneaking something in?"

Just then, Specs's head emerged from the river right in front of Frederick. He spit a mouthful of water into Frederick's face. Frederick sputtered and reversed in the water as far as the ring of boys would allow.

Specs laughed. "Gosh you're funny, Dash," he said. Specs's laugh didn't sound like the one from breakfast, though. This laugh made Frederick flinch. "You know," Specs said, "my brother always talked like you were some kind of legend. But you're just a normal guy."

Frederick's feet kicked to keep his head above

the surface. He didn't say anything. He was aware of the other boys, listening in.

"Maybe that's always how it is with legends," Specs said. "Maybe they're never as cool in real life." His tone was philosophical, but the gleam in his eyes was steely.

"Maybe *I'm* even wilder than you are," said Specs. It was a challenge. Frederick wanted to know when being "wild" had become such a great thing. It suddenly seemed like being "wild" was just the best thing ever, and Frederick hadn't been part of the committee that voted to make it that way. He hadn't had a say in it, and now he just had to go with it.

"Maybe," Frederick said. "But maybe you're not." He didn't know why he was challenging Specs back, except he had to say something, and it felt like the natural thing to do.

Specs sank low in the water, all the way to his eyes. Then he lifted his chin up. "So who did you want to call?" he asked.

"It's personal business," Frederick said, trying to sound tough, but he thought it came out sounding fussy. He tried again. "It's my personal, private business." It was hard to sound tough while your legs were kicking furiously and your arms were treading water.

As more and more of the campers gathered around to listen, Frederick realized his mistake. Whenever people found out that you had a secret, they worked to shake it out of you like a Butterfinger caught in a vending machine's coils.

Frederick needed to give them an answer fast so they would leave him alone. He tried to think of someone the scary Dashiell Blackwood might reasonably call, but the only people he could think of were his mom, his dad, his grandma Sue, Sarah Anne, and the police.

"Anyway," he said, "it doesn't matter because Nosebleed says there's no service." He hoped that would settle it.

"Are you calling your glasses-wearing friend, Raj?" Specs asked.

"*No,*" said Frederick. He felt a pang of guilt that he'd given Raj's name to a criminally evil boy. He could imagine one day, months from now, when Specs tracked Raj down, broke into his bedroom at night, and snapped his eyeglasses "in twain" while Raj slept. And it would be Frederick's fault. When the investigators questioned how Specs had found out about Raj, Frederick was going to have to act just as confused as everyone else.

"Well, there's a landline," Specs said casually. "You could use that to call out."

"There is?" Frederick said cautiously.

"Yeah," said Specs. "But it's in Eric's office. And we're not allowed in there."

"Oh," said Frederick. His arms and legs churned.

"I'll help you break in, though." Specs flipped over in the water, twisting like an eel. "If you're not scared."

10

A Little Horse's Toothbrush

FREDERICK DIDN'T WANT TO BREAK INTO ERIC'S OFFICE. He *really* didn't want to break into Eric's office with Specs. What he wanted was to just drop the whole breaking-into-the-office thing and forget about it. Unfortunately, that was impossible.

"Let's do it now," Specs kept saying throughout the day.

It seemed like he was at Frederick's elbow every second—during lunch, on the "character-building" afternoon hike, while they were learning to tie knots and do other "aggression-relieving" crafts. Having Specs hiss into his ear, his breath hot on Frederick's neck, was annoying and a little frightening, and it made it impossible for Frederick to figure out how he was going to get out of this situation and back home, where he belonged.

"*Now*," Specs whispered at dinner. "It's a golden opportunity."

"No," Frederick whispered back. "Later. Too many people watching." He stabbed a Vienna sausage on a bent-tined fork and looked sadly at it. Miss Betty was gone, and Merle, the cook who had replaced her, didn't arrange all the food neatly in the serving trays. Frederick didn't think there would be s'mores.

"Nobody's watching," Specs said. "Everyone's right here. Eric's cabin is deserted."

"He'll probably go to his office after he eats," Frederick said, inventing yet another reason why they couldn't break in to use the phone.

The Professor, Nosebleed, and Ant Bite were silent. They had been silent on the matter ever since the river. They looked at Frederick with pity but kept their mouths shut. He didn't blame them. He thought they were smart. He should've kept his mouth shut a lot more in his life, and maybe he wouldn't be here right now.

"I'll go with you," Specs said. "I'll be your lookout. And then you can call your buddy on the outside."

Frederick knew that Specs knew that he wasn't going to call some "buddy on the outside," that he wasn't going to call some contact who would sneak him in contraband. Frederick suspected that Specs also knew that Frederick really did want to call his mommy. Frederick knew that Specs knew, and Specs knew that Frederick knew that he knew. Everybody knew, and yet they kept pretending that they didn't.

It was like they were playing some complicated game where Specs and Frederick both had to *pretend* that Frederick was going to make a potentially illegal phone call. Frederick would lose the game if he admitted that he wasn't calling someone scary or shady. He would also lose if he told Specs to drop it because he had decided not to make a phone call after all. And Specs would win when he helped Frederick break into the office and listened in on Frederick's phone call with his mommy.

Basically, there was no way for Frederick to win, so really, all he was doing was postponing the moment when he lost. It was a horrible game, and Frederick didn't know how he'd wound up playing it, but here he was.

"Well, when *are* you going to be ready, *Ding-a-Ling*?" Specs asked.

"Later, *Specs*," Frederick answered.

"Yeah, right," Specs said.

"That *is* right," Frederick said, putting an end to the conversation.

"You're not going to do it," Specs said.

"Yes," Frederick said. "I am, too."

"Not," Specs muttered under his breath.

After dinner, when the sun was sinking behind the pine trees, the campers went to their sleeping cabins.

It was the first time Frederick had seen the inside of Group Thirteen's cabin. It was one large room that smelled like fresh air, cedar, and barf. A moth fluttered against the bare lightbulb in the middle of the low ceiling. There were three beds on one side of the room and two on the other. Four of the beds already had sheets on them. Nosebleed, the Professor, Ant Bite, and Specs each went to one of the made beds and collapsed.

"*Urgf*," Nosebleed groaned.

The Professor's feet hung off the end of his bed,

and his head bumped the wall. He didn't seem to care. He opened his book and put it over his eyes to block out the light.

Specs picked dead beetles off his bed and flung them at Ant Bite.

The fifth, unmade bed had a folded stack of thread-bare sheets on top of a stained mattress. The stain was shaped like a face with its mouth open, scream-ing in terror. At the end of the cabin was a porcelain sink with a dripping faucet. Frederick walked over to it and fiddled with the single tap. A slick of red algae rimmed the drain. While Frederick was taking all this in, Benjamin's voice called from outside.

"Dash! I found you some stuff in the lost and found!" Their counselor lumbered into the cabin, carrying a cardboard box that he dropped on Fred-erick's bed.

Frederick went over to the box. He pulled out an extra-large red jersey and sniffed it gingerly. It smelled like cabbage. He dropped it on the mattress and peeled off his own nasty shirt. The jersey's sleeves were so big they went past his elbows. The tail fell al-most to his knees, like a dress. But at least it didn't have blood on it.

Then he looked back into the cardboard box and pulled out a yellow flashlight just like the one they had at home, only this one contained dead batteries. He also found a pair of men's loafers, mismatched socks, a book about girl spies, and a green-handled toothbrush.

"You don't have to use that," Benjamin said, pointing at the toothbrush Frederick was holding. "I just saw it and thought of you." He laughed. "How you were worried about your teeth," he added.

The toothbrush's bristles were not tight and straight like a fresh-out-of-the-package toothbrush. They were gray and splayed and flattened.

"Whose toothbrush *was* this?" Frederick asked. "It looks like someone brushed a horse's teeth with it."

"Why would anyone brush a horse's teeth?" the Professor mumbled behind the pages of his book.

"A horse would have a bigger toothbrush," Ant Bite said, sitting up on his bed.

"What would *you* know about it?" Specs said, flicking another beetle at him.

Ant Bite glared at him and lay down, rolling over to face the wall.

"Maybe it was a little tiny horse," Nosebleed said.

He lifted his arms and held his two pointer fingers apart to indicate a three-inch-tall horse.

"Yeah, you don't have to use it," Benjamin said again, turning pink. "Like I said, I just thought of our earlier conversation." He gave another laugh. "Actually, maybe you *shouldn't* use it."

"You think?" said Specs.

Benjamin took the toothbrush out of Frederick's hand and tossed it at the metal trash can by the door. He missed, and it clattered to the floor.

"Good night, campers!" Benjamin said. "I'll see you tomorrow." He walked out of the cabin with a bounce in his step and closed the door behind him.

They could still hear Benjamin's humming when Specs rolled off his bed and took a step toward Frederick.

"Now," Specs said, narrowing his eyes.

At some point that day, Frederick had realized that the reason Specs squinted all the time was because he couldn't see clearly, because he really did need "spectacles," so it was a shame that he'd snapped his in twain.

"Not *now*," Frederick said.

"Then when?" Specs said. "You've put it off all day. You're not going to do it."

"When everyone's asleep," Frederick said, and he deliberately rolled his eyes. That was how fed up he was with Specs. He was so sick of him that he was forgetting to be scared.

"One hour." Specs tapped the face of the digital watch he wore.

"One hour," Frederick agreed, not because he thought that was a good time but because he was tired of arguing.

After sleeping for only a few hours in a boat and then spending the day climbing a rope, swimming, hiking, and being scared out of his mind, Frederick was too exhausted to put the sheets on his bed properly. He dropped the fitted sheet on the floor and spread the top sheet so that it mostly covered the stain. Then he picked up his feet and fell face-first on the bed. He was asleep before his eyelids were all the way closed.

The next thing Frederick knew, someone was slapping the back of his head. Frederick groaned and tried to turn away from the slapping.

"It's time, Ding-a-Ling," Specs said. He held his

watch right up to Frederick's nose. According to the green-glowing face, it was ten thirty.

Frederick wanted to go back to sleep more than he'd ever wanted anything in his life. But he put his hands on the bed and pushed himself up.

Later, Frederick would marvel at the super-human strength it took to wake himself from the deepest sleep he'd ever experienced to sneak across a camp for not-yet-transformed boys to try to break into a seriously creepy dude's office. And he would know that he found that strength deep within himself *not* because he was afraid of Specs (though he *was* afraid of Specs), and *not* because he wanted to call his mom to come pick him up (though he really, really hoped that he would get to do that). No. He was able to get up because he knew that if he didn't, Specs would say he had chickened out, and Frederick didn't want to give him the satis-faction.

He stood up with his knees bumping into the edge of his mattress. He patted himself like he was check-ing his pockets. His tennis shoes were still on his feet; he hadn't taken them off before falling asleep. He was wearing the baggy red jersey. He had no other possessions except some loafers, a dead flashlight, and a girl spy book, so he decided that he was ready to go. He stumbled through the dark cabin, past the others' beds. He opened the door and stepped out into the night, catching his shoulder on the doorjamb.

"Dang it," he muttered, rubbing his shoulder.

"*Dang it*," Specs mimicked Frederick, and snickered. "Is that the best you can do?"

"You kiss your mama with that mouth?" Nosebleed chuckled at his own joke.

The Professor, Nosebleed, and Ant Bite had also risen and were now following Frederick and Specs out of the cabin. Apparently, they were going with them to Eric's office, and that seemed right to Frederick. They were a group. They were going to do this together.

Specs was right on Frederick's heels as he crossed the camp, sticking to the dark patches and staying out of the yellow glow beneath the floodlights attached to the buildings. The moon was bright tonight, and Frederick was able to make out his feet and a bit of the ground in front of him.

The head counselor's office was a tiny cabin that

was just off the main building. It faced the small parking lot where Frederick had first spotted the school bus and the campers. It was brighter here because the parking lot didn't have so many trees blocking the moonlight.

Group Thirteen huddled close together in front of Eric's office. The lights were off inside. The head counselor must've already gone to his sleeping cabin . . . Frederick hoped.

Specs and Frederick were the only ones still in their day clothes. The other three were wearing pajamas. Nosebleed and Ant Bite had put on tennis shoes with their striped pants. The Professor was barefoot.

Specs reached out and shoved Frederick's arm. Frederick stepped away from the group.

The two wooden steps that led to the porch were so rotten that each one sagged under his weight when he climbed. He stood in front of the door for a moment, listening hard, every sense on high alert, expecting Eric to materialize at any moment. Eric, in his too-tight shorts and his sunglasses, because Frederick got the feeling that Eric wore his sunglasses all the time, even in the dark, probably because he didn't have eyes. Because he was a cyborg.

"What are you waiting for?" Specs whispered from where the others stood.

Frederick shook himself out of his daydream. Then he took a deep breath, grabbed the doorknob, and turned.

Nothing happened. Frederick jostled the doorknob and tried turning it again, but it was locked tight.

He twisted to whisper over his shoulder. "Now what?" He had never broken into anywhere before, and now that he had tried the front door, he was out of ideas.

Nosebleed, Specs, the Professor, and Ant Bite all climbed onto the porch.

"Did you think it would just be unlocked?" Specs asked.

"Yes," Frederick said, nodding.

He had. He had thought that he would open the door and go into Eric's office and use the phone, and that would be a wrong thing to do because the campers weren't allowed in there. He hadn't thought they would actually have to *break into* the place, like

Mission Impossible–type stuff. Maybe he should've brought along the spy book after all. Maybe he could've gotten some pointers.

The others held a furious, whispered conversation, most of which Frederick missed because he had leaned against the cabin wall and fallen into a doze while he was still standing.

"We can pop the hinges out," Ant Bite said in a determined voice that cut through Frederick's slumber. Ant Bite was pointing at the edge of the door.

Frederick and the others turned to look at the hinges at the top and bottom. Frederick had never really noticed door hinges before. Were they on all doors? He guessed they must be.

"How are we gonna do that?" Nosebleed asked, rubbing the side of his head and gazing at the hinges in bewilderment, like he'd never noticed them either.

"A screwdriver and a hammer." Ant Bite shrugged.

"Have you *got* a screwdriver and a hammer?" Specs asked.

Ant Bite shrugged again.

"Exactly," Specs said.

"Well then, you've got to break the glass if you want to get in there," Ant Bite said, gesturing at the window beside the door. Through the window Frederick could see a desk with stacks of paper, all arranged in perfect piles, and on the corner of the desk, a big, old-fashioned telephone.

"If they find out you did it, they'll kick you out for sure," Nosebleed warned. "They'll call the police."

"They wouldn't call the police. And they aren't going to find out," Specs insisted. "None of us are gonna tell."

Annoyance flashed through Frederick.

None of us are gonna tell translated into *Somebody for sure is going to tell*. And then the person who got told on always said, *You promised you wouldn't tell*. And the person who told was all like, *No, I didn't*.

"Can't we . . . I don't know," Frederick said. "Can't we pick the lock?"

"Can you pick a lock?" Nosebleed asked hopefully.

"No," said Frederick.

"Then no," Nosebleed said, shaking his head.

"Break it," Specs said.

Frederick hesitated.

"It's just a piece of glass," Specs urged.

Nosebleed, Ant Bite, and the Professor didn't say anything, but their silence roared in Frederick's ears.

Frederick had never broken a window before. He'd never broken anything on purpose. He'd broken stuff by accident plenty of times. But breaking Eric's office window would be different. It would be mean. And wrong.

Frederick might have been a flea. He might have been a flounder and a ding-a-ling. But he wasn't a bad person. Not yet. But maybe it was unavoidable. Maybe someone who screwed up as much as he did was bound to screw up at being a good person, too. The thought made Frederick sad. He didn't want to become a bad person. He wasn't going to let that happen, he decided. At least, not tonight.

He turned away from the window and climbed down the sagging steps to the ground.

"So you're not going to do it after all," Specs said from the porch. "I knew you wouldn't." There was triumph in his voice.

Even though the day had been hot, the air was cool now that the sun had set. Frederick tucked his fists in his armpits and squeezed his arms tight around himself. "I didn't say I wasn't doing it," he said.

And then without really thinking about it, he started walking through the parking lot toward the two-lane road that led away from camp. After the first few steps, he began walking with more purpose. If he didn't go back to the cabin, then Specs couldn't say he had given up yet. He was just taking a break.

"What are you doing?" Nosebleed called after him.

"I'm taking a break!" Frederick called with some anger.

"*Shh!*" the others all shushed from the porch.

Behind him he heard the Professor swear softly, and then he heard the slapping of footsteps as the others ran to catch up with him.

11

The Constellation Fleaus Tinyus

THE LIGHTS FROM CAMP HAD SHRUNK TO NO MORE THAN twinkles in the trees behind them, and they were still walking down the dark road.

"What are we doing out here, Dash?" the Professor asked—not for the first time.

"We're *walking*!" Frederick answered loudly.

"*Shh!*" Nosebleed, Specs, the Professor, and Ant Bite shushed him.

They walked in silence for a while.

"Why don't we go back to camp now?" Nosebleed suggested, a plaintive whine in his voice.

"I don't want to go back to camp," Frederick insisted. "I want to walk."

At first, Frederick had started walking because he was trying to get away from Eric's cabin and delay the moment when the others realized once and for all that Dash (or Frederick) wasn't the fearless cool guy that he'd pretended to be.

But as the night air filled his lungs, his feet had fallen into a rhythm, and the high-pitched chirring of the cicadas and the squelching bellows of the bullfrogs had gotten so loud and frequent that it melded into a single night sound, lulling Frederick into a trancelike state. It was like, as long as he was walking, he didn't have to think about any of his problems. He didn't have to worry about Eric or about how his mom was probably going to be mad at him for getting lost or how when he went back to his regular life he was still going to be the same old flea-like Frederick. He wished he could keep walking forever, but eventually, his legs slowed like a windup toy grinding to a halt, and he stopped.

The others walked a few steps before they realized he wasn't moving anymore.

"We're going back now?" Nosebleed squeaked.

"My legs are tired," Frederick announced, and he

sat down right there on the pavement, stretched his legs straight in front of him, and lay back, letting his arms flop at his sides.

The pavement radiated heat that was left over from the sun, and the warmth soaked into Frederick's spine. The back of one hand rested against the painted yellow line. His chest rose and fell steadily. Above him, the sky was littered with more stars than he'd ever seen before.

Frederick had never lain in the middle of a road. "This is weirdly comfortable," he said.

One of the boys sighed. Then somebody was sitting down beside Frederick and stretching out.

"Should we be lying in the middle of a road?" Nosebleed asked when all five of them were sprawled out across the asphalt like accident victims.

Nobody answered.

"What are we going to do if a car comes?" Nosebleed said more insistently.

"Get up?" the Professor suggested. "Move out of the way?"

"We'd see the headlights before it got here," Ant Bite said.

They were silent for a few moments.

"I wish I was in my bed," Nosebleed said in a small voice.

"I wish I never had to go to school again." The Professor sighed.

"I wish I could make the Iron Man suit," Ant Bite said. "Like, for real, and then I'd fly wherever I wanted to go."

"That's stupid," Specs said.

"No, it isn't," Ant Bite snapped.

Then Frederick said, "I wish I was on a cruise."

"A *cruise*." Specs snorted. "What do you know about a cruise?"

"I've been on lots of cruises," Frederick said. "I would go down the waterslide ten times," he said. "And then I would go up to the bar and get a strawberry daiquiri."

His eyelids fell shut as he imagined it. The sun, giant and blazing in the sky. Steel-drum music so energetic that you could almost see the shiny sounds bouncing off the deck. The smell of coconut oil sunscreen. A frozen drink and a brain-freeze headache.

"And the chocolate fountain at the midnight buffet," Frederick murmured.

"There's no such thing as a chocolate fountain," Specs said.

"Yes, there is," said Nosebleed. "When my sister got married, there was a chocolate fountain at the reception."

"So . . ." Specs's voice was frustrated. "So do they drain the water and put the chocolate in? Do they clean it first?"

"It's not a real fountain. It's small," Nosebleed explained. "Like a little fountain that sits on a table, and it's just for chocolate."

"'S'not what a cruise is, though," Frederick said, his words slurring together. "The daiquiris and fountains and beach . . .'s'all good. But what a cruise really *is* . . . is a chance to get away. Get away from all your problems."

The boys were quiet for a long time.

"Swear on your mom's life there's a chocolate fountain," Specs demanded.

Frederick sighed. Normally, he refused to swear anything on his mom's life because if it turned out that he was making a mistake, he didn't want to have accidentally killed her. But in this case, Frederick—even in his confused, sleep-drunk state—knew what he was talking about.

He lifted one heavy arm and let his hand plop down over his heart like he was reciting the Pledge of Allegiance. "I swear to you on my mother's life," he said, "there are chocolate fountains."

A moment of silence followed this pronouncement.

"You know what I did to get sent to Omigoshee?" the Professor said suddenly.

"What?" Frederick asked.

"I didn't try out for the middle school football team." The Professor's voice was quiet, not traveling farther than the five of them as he spoke.

Frederick wondered how not trying out for football was bad enough to get you sent to Camp Omigoshee. He had assumed that the boys who were sent to disciplinary camp had done something really, really bad.

The Professor went on. "I had a growth spurt at the end of last school year. Seven inches in three months. I ate so many bologna sandwiches. And the coach at school—he kept telling me I've got to join the team, I've got to try out.

"'Don't just think of yourself,'" the Professor said in a gruff growl, like he was imitating the coach. "'Think of what you can do for your school.'" Then he sighed. "But I don't want to be on the team. I like

to *watch* football and I like to read. That's it. So I never put my name on the sign-up sheet and didn't go to the first tryout. The next thing I know, the guidance counselor sends a letter to my parents about how I won't participate at school because I have a bad attitude and maybe I should go to this camp . . ." His voice trailed off.

"What did your parents do?" Ant Bite asked. "I mean, they took your side, right?"

"No. They sent me here, didn't they?" the Professor said. He didn't sound angry, just resigned.

"Do you guys want to know what I did to get sent here?" Specs asked eagerly.

"No," Frederick and Ant Bite said together.

"Not really," the Professor said.

"I want to know," Nosebleed's voice called.

"I broke somebody's glasses," Specs said, and then paused.

Frederick sighed.

"I broke my *teacher's* glasses," Specs said with a note of awe in his voice, like he couldn't believe it himself.

Nobody said anything for a while.

"Did you hear what I said?" Specs demanded.

The Professor grunted. "How do we know you're not just saying that?" he asked. "You may just want us to think you're tough."

"I did do it!" Specs insisted. "How do we know you're not just saying all that stuff about football, huh?"

"We should do it," Ant Bite said suddenly. "We should go on a cruise."

"Us?" Frederick said, and his first thought was that there was no way any of them would ever go anywhere together. But then, to his surprise, he found that he could easily imagine being on a cruise with Nosebleed, the Professor, Ant Bite, and even Specs. They were all in lounge chairs with strawberry daiquiris. All careening down the waterslide. If Frederick had imagined going on a cruise with the boys from Group Thirteen earlier in the day, he would've been terrified. But now, with all of them sprawled out on the asphalt, he wasn't afraid at all. Today had actually been kind of fun. While he had been climbing the rope or swimming or arguing with Specs, it hadn't felt particularly fun. But looking back on it, he realized that it *had* been. Even arguing with Specs. Frederick had felt like he was a part of something, like he belonged.

"Yeah," Frederick said. "That'd be great."

"Let's go, then," Ant Bite said. "Let's go now."

"We'd get in trouble," Nosebleed said. "We're not supposed to leave camp. We're not even supposed to be out *here*."

"It'd be worth it," the Professor said at once. "To get to go on a cruise, it'd be worth it."

"The counselors would send out a search party for us," Nosebleed said. "Call our families and tell 'em we were missing."

"We could slash their tires," Ant Bite suggested quickly.

"And smash the telephone," Specs added. "If Dash wasn't too scared."

"I'm not scared," Frederick protested groggily.

"And then they couldn't follow us or tell on us," Ant Bite finished.

Frederick opened his eyes and let his head fall sideways so he could look at the younger boy. Ant Bite's eyes were closed. And for the first time since Frederick had met him, he looked happy. Happy at the thought of slashing tires, but still . . . it was nice.

"How will we get there, though?" Specs asked.

Frederick pointed his face toward the stars again

and closed his eyes. "Take Interstate 16 until you get to 95. Then go south all the way to Port Verde Shoals."

"Are we really going to do it?" Nosebleed asked.

"*I'm* not scared," Specs said.

"Let's do it," the Professor said. "Let's do it for real."

Frederick didn't know how long Group Thirteen lay in the road beneath the glittering stars, soaking up the heat from the pavement and imagining every detail of their dream vacation. He just knew that at some point that night, the others got up, and Nosebleed and the Professor, being the biggest, hauled him to his feet and draped his arms over their shoulders, and they staggered back to their cabin and to a peaceful slumber.

12

A Failure to Communicate

FREDERICK'S MOM WAS HUGE. WAY, WAY TOO BIG. OR maybe Frederick was too small. Yeah, that was it. He was the size of an actual flea, and his mom was coming at him, her gigantic feet making the earth shudder beneath him.

"Mom?" Frederick said.

She was shaking a can of Raid, the metal ball inside it clacking against the container.

"Mom! Don't spray me!" Frederick shouted. "It's me! Frederick!"

But she didn't hear him.

"Everything's ready," Ant Bite's voice said. "You've got to wake up."

"No!" Frederick yelled, and the walls of his nightmare collapsed like a house of cards.

Then someone was shaking his shoulder, and he opened his eyes to see that daylight filled the cabin, and Ant Bite actually *was* standing over him and speaking.

"'Kay." Frederick yawned hugely. "Wake up," he repeated, and on autopilot, his body pushed itself up and swung his legs over the side of the bed. He groaned as he straightened out his stiff back . . . and arms . . . and legs. The mattress was almost as uncomfortable as sleeping in the bottom of Mr. Mincey's boat.

"We slashed the tires on all the trucks," Ant Bite said.

"*Mugh?*" Frederick moaned through another yawn.

"And cut the phone line," Ant Bite said.

"Gosh, that must've been hard work," Frederick said with admiration, and then he crashed backward on the bed and fell asleep again.

"Hey." Ant Bite snapped his fingers in front of Frederick's face. "Are you awake?"

"*Nuh-uh,*" Frederick said. He wasn't awake. He'd gone from one nightmare to a different one where

Ant Bite was admitting to committing some terrible crime. *That was so stressful*, Frederick thought.

"Wake *up*," Ant Bite said. "Do you hear me? We've got everything ready to go."

Frederick was slowly realizing that he was not asleep and this was not a dream. Ant Bite—the real Ant Bite and not dream Ant Bite—had just told him that they'd slashed the tires and cut the phone line.

Frederick clutched a handful of his thin sheet. Then he opened his eyes and waited for Ant Bite to come into focus.

"You cut the phone line," Frederick said from the safety of his mattress.

Ant Bite nodded.

"And you slashed the tires," Frederick said.

"And we broke into Eric's office and got some supplies." Ant Bite nodded again.

"But why?" Frederick said. "Why would you do that?"

Ant Bite tilted his head to the side in confusion. "We've been getting everything ready," he said. "To go on the cruise," he added when Frederick didn't respond.

"We?" Frederick sat up, still clutching his sheet, and looked around the cabin.

The Professor was stuffing socks into the corners of an already-full duffel bag. Specs was standing beside the window, peering out at the yard beyond like he was keeping lookout. Nosebleed sat on the edge of his bed with a worried wrinkle between his eyes. He had a fat backpack, the straps already over his shoulders.

"You think we're going on a cruise," Frederick said as he started to understand. "Today," he said. "You think we're going on a cruise today."

Frederick's memories of the night before were fuzzy around the edges. But obviously somewhere along the way there had been a massive misunderstanding. He had thought—no, he had *known* that what they were doing last night was fantasizing about running away to go on a cruise, imagining something they were *never going to do*.

Now Ant Bite was standing beside Frederick's bed. He held the strap of a small shoulder bag out to Frederick.

"I packed your stuff," he said. "We even found some batteries for your flashlight."

"Eric's nose-hair trimmers had double As," Specs said gleefully from his station by the window.

The Professor lifted a finger and smiled. "*Had*," he said. Frederick scrambled off the bed and backed away from the bag like it held live spiders.

"We can't . . . We can't just *go*," Frederick said.

"Why not?" the Professor asked.

"Why not," Frederick repeated faintly. And there were so many reasons *why not* that his brain had a system overload as it tried to process them all.

For starters, they needed to eat breakfast. And after breakfast, what were they going to do . . . *walk* to Port Verde Shoals? It took six freaking hours for Frederick's dad to *drive* there. And who knew which direction the interstate was from here? Not Frederick! What were they supposed to eat and how were they supposed to survive while they were traveling? How were five kids going to get on board a cruise ship without tickets and papers?

Frederick imagined sneaking onto the cruise. He imagined a voice yelling over a megaphone, *Catch those kids!* And security people in small shorts and flashing sunglasses chasing him belowdecks until he wound up hiding in the boiler room, wedged in the giant gears of a cruise ship engine, bilge rats leaping off the floor trying to nip whatever bit of him they could reach.

In Group Thirteen's cabin, Frederick was panting as if he could hear the rats' teeth clicking right then.

"Okay . . . ," he said, trying to sound reasonable. "Last night we enjoyed *talking* about going on vacation. We enjoyed *imagining* it. But we can't actually *do* it." This made sense to Frederick. What the guys were suggesting was flat-out impossible.

When Frederick had first arrived at Camp Omigo-shee and decided to stay, it was because he'd thought, for one moment, that he could do something like that. Like he, Frederick Frederickson, could have an adventure and become someone special. He'd been wrong. People like him—fleas—they didn't do things like that. Adventures didn't work out for them.

He looked at the others, expecting to see the effect of his words, expecting to see their excitement dim as they realized he was right.

Their expectant faces looked right back at him, *un*dimmed, and Frederick realized a crucial mistake in his reasoning. *He* couldn't have an adventure. These guys, though, had gotten up before dawn so they could slash tires, break a window, steal the batteries from a man's nose-hair trimmers, and cut off an entire camp from civilization. And now they were ready to go on vacation.

"Oh, brother," Frederick said, looking at their faces. He shook his head to clear it.

Maybe this was why he didn't have real best friends. Because when the time came to have an adventure or do something awesome, they were all ready to go, and he wasn't able to follow. He couldn't keep up, couldn't hang. The guys in Group Thirteen were about to realize that, and then Frederick would be back where he started. Alone.

"Dash is right," Nosebleed said suddenly. "What if we get caught?"

"Yes," Frederick said, "exactly!"

"So what if we get caught?" Specs said. "Are you scared of getting caught?"

"No!" Nosebleed shifted, and the bedsprings creaked beneath him.

Specs tapped the plastic wand that opened and closed the blinds and threw Nosebleed one of his practiced sneers.

"It's just . . ." Nosebleed hitched the straps of the backpack up. "I've never been in trouble before."

"You've never been in trouble?" Frederick said. "Then why are you even here?"

Nosebleed shrugged. "My grandma and teacher thought I'd like camp. They thought I could do this weekend camp and see if I like it before I do a long summer camp next year. Like a test run." He paused. "And I do like it."

"It's a discipline camp!" Frederick said. "Why'd you come to a discipline camp?"

"It's more like a transformational camp," the Professor said. "Like a personal development thing."

"You should stay," Ant Bite said to Nosebleed.

Nosebleed looked relieved.

"But I'm going," Ant Bite said.

"*I'm* going," Specs said quickly, as if someone had suggested that he was too scared to go.

"I want to see the chocolate fountain," the Professor said, as if that made his decision.

Nosebleed slid the straps of his backpack off his shoulders.

"And I can cover for you," he said, back to his cheerful self. "I'll say that you're all in here throwing up and it smells terrible so no one can come in, and that'll buy you a little more time."

The Professor nodded and zipped up his bag with a jerk.

"They've found out about the trucks," Specs said sharply. His eyes were narrowed as he peered out the window.

Frederick was in his socks. His shoes were on the floor by his bed. Had he taken them off last night? He didn't remember.

He sat down on the floor and stuffed his feet into his shoes.

"Finally," Ant Bite said, watching Frederick. "Let's do this!"

Frederick didn't answer, letting Ant Bite think he was putting on his shoes so he could run away. He pushed himself to his feet and headed for the door. Things had gone too far. He couldn't run away from camp! He couldn't hike to Port Verde Shoals without an adult. He couldn't because . . . he couldn't. He'd had enough, and it was time to go home. He would find Benjamin and *make* him understand that he was Frederick Frederickson. He'd tell him things only the real Frederick would know.

"Hey, wait up!" Ant Bite called.

Frederick opened the door and stepped onto the narrow porch. A blur flashed across his vision, and the next thing he knew, a rubber ball was slamming into his stomach.

"Errrf." Frederick doubled over. His knees hit the porch boards.

"Rise and shine, maggots!" a voice said.

Frederick clutched his stomach and looked up. Eric

stood in front of their cabin, legs planted wide, sunglasses flashing.

The ball that had hit Frederick rolled off the edge of the porch and bounced away—*thunk, thunk, thunk.*

"We're playing dodgeball this morning," Eric said.

13

Dodgeball, Again

FREDERICK WAS NAUSEATED. OR WAS THE RIGHT WORD *nauseous*? He didn't know. Was there a word for when your guts were trying to claw their way out of your throat so they could drag themselves away and leave you to face your impending doom alone?

He and the boys from Group Thirteen joined a straggling band of campers heading across the grounds. Eric had a ball tucked under each arm, and he jogged up to the next cabin and kicked the door open, yelling, "Wake up, campers! You stay up all night destroying property, you must not need sleep!"

More bleary-eyed, sleep-tousled boys staggered out into the morning sunlight.

Dodgeball. Dodgeball again. The *crunch* of his

nose breaking. A shudder shook through Frederick as he remembered the pain.

His legs were as heavy as if he had a sandbag tied to each ankle. He looked around, trying to find some way out. In the distance he saw two counselors hurrying from the main building to the head counselor's cabin. One of them had her head tilted toward a walkie-talkie. They were probably dealing with the crisis of the slashed tires, cut phone line, and stolen nose-hair-trimmer batteries. Frederick casually started to veer in the counselors' direction, thinking he could tell them everything and get this sorted out, preferably *before* he had to play dodgeball. But as he broke away from the group, Nosebleed, the Professor, and Ant Bite automatically headed that way, too, sticking close to him.

Frederick tried to shoo them off, but they gave him confused looks.

"Back in line, boys!" Eric barked, hustling up beside them to steer them back into the pack.

"Hey, you forgot to call us maggots," Nosebleed said.

Eric's face turned dangerously red, and they hurried past him. Frederick looked back over his shoulder just as the counselors disappeared into the cabin.

The boys walked to the far side of the camp and stopped at the edge of a football field. Except, Frederick corrected himself mentally, this field didn't have any chalk lines . . . or a scoreboard . . . or goalposts. Actually, the field was just a rectangular area of grass with big bald spots where the sand showed through. Four wooden posts, painted orange, marked each corner. So it wasn't a football field at all, but it didn't matter to Frederick if he humiliated himself on NFL-standard turf or this mangy patch of grass.

Even after the disastrous rope-climbing relay, a lot of the boys at camp still thought Dash was cool. Or they thought that he was a little bit cool. But they were about to see the real Frederick.

"Atomic dodgeball!" Eric shouted, striding down the line of boys. "That's what we're going to play this morning!"

Frederick's nauseous/nauseated stomach flopped over. Ant Bite sidled up to him in line. He nudged Frederick with his elbow.

"Hey," Ant Bite whispered. "We could sneak off once the game starts. Everybody'll be running around. We can go through those woods." He nodded at the thick trees on the other side of the field. Then he looked at Frederick's face and leaned back. "Seriously," he said, "what is wrong with you? You look like you're gonna be sick."

"*Hmmph*," Frederick humphed. "I have a . . . a dodgeball problem," he whispered.

The others all listened while pretending to pay attention to Eric, who was explaining the rules of atomic dodgeball (the rules were . . . there were no rules).

"I had a bad experience," Frederick said, barely moving his lips so that his words wouldn't carry. "I don't know if I can play."

"So you have, like, a phobia?" the Professor suggested in a low voice.

Frederick swallowed and shrugged.

Specs crossed his arms and looked at the ground to hide his mouth as he spoke. "I've never heard of a *dodgeball* phobia."

"You can develop a phobia for anything," the Professor said.

"Dodgeball's fun," Nosebleed argued. "You'll see, Dash," he said encouragingly.

"No talking!" Eric roared, stalking down the line toward them.

They all stood up straight and stared ahead.

"Dash!" Eric barked. He stopped right in front of Frederick, so close that Frederick could smell him. He smelled like sweat and villainy. "Have you got a problem?"

"No, sir," Frederick said.

"Why don't you start us off," Eric said with a smile that showed large, square teeth.

Frederick didn't answer. He wished he knew why Eric had decided to hate *him* in particular. Maybe it was his mission in life to stamp out all the fleas, and he could sense that Frederick was one.

"Here." Eric shoved one of the balls into Frederick's stomach, knocking the wind out of him for the second time that morning.

Then he strode down the line. Ant Bite, Nosebleed, and the Professor all turned to look at Frederick with questions written on their faces.

"Nobody has a dodgeball phobia," Specs muttered. "That's stupid."

A minute later Eric blew his whistle, and the boys jogged out onto the field. Frederick stayed on the edge, holding the ball between his hands. His thumbs rubbed across the ripples and whorls stamped in the rubber. The boys were spreading out.

Okay, Frederick told himself. *Pull yourself together. You can do this.*

He'd only played dodgeball twice in his life. Once at a family reunion and once at school. He'd broken his nose 50 percent of the time he'd played. Statistically speaking, there was a 50 percent chance he was about to break his nose . . . again. He thought of Candace Licky, the girl who'd nearly died playing dodgeball. Maybe that would be him this time.

Here goes, he thought, and he lifted one foot and put it onto the field. Most of the boys moved as far as possible from Frederick and from the other boy Eric had given a ball to. A handful of boys, though, stayed close, almost within range of a thrown dodgeball. They paced back and forth in front of Frederick, their eyes gleaming with challenge.

Eric's whistle blew again, shattering Frederick's nerves.

The boys took off, running in every direction. The other boy who had a ball drew his arm way back and hurled it like Thor flinging his hammer. The ball slammed into a kid's chest, knocking him flat on his back.

No one stopped to check on the boy. Someone dashed in and picked up the ball that was bouncing along the ground.

Frederick clutched his own ball to his body. He hadn't moved. He was standing there, panting.

"What are you doing?" the Professor called to him, running closer. "Throw the ball!" He jogged smoothly and easily. He looked like a natural athlete, and Frederick could see why his coach wanted him to play football. "Throw it!" the Professor shouted.

Frederick ran a few steps forward. He lifted the ball over his head. Boys were running in every direction. Frederick threw wildly. The ball hit the ground three feet in front of his shoes and rolled away.

A boy swooped in and scooped up the free ball. Then he whipped his head around, looking right at Frederick.

Frederick's whole body tensed, bracing for impact.

But . . . the boy *nodded* at Frederick and yelled, "Hey, watch this, Dash!" And he ran off, throwing the ball at someone else as he went.

Frederick was so relieved that his knees started

to buckle, but then someone grabbed his arm and was dragging him along.

"What are you doing?" the Professor said in his ear. "Run." He shoved Frederick hard.

Frederick ran then. He zigged and zagged around the other boys, his heart galloping.

Someone bumped into him, or he bumped into them—he couldn't tell.

"Sorry, Dash!" the boy yelled after crashing into Frederick.

Frederick didn't answer. He didn't have any breath to speak. He looked over his shoulder to see the boy running off, rubbing his arm where he'd clipped Frederick. When Frederick turned around, he locked eyes with a boy who was right in front of him, arm drawn back, a ball in his hand.

Frederick jerked to a stop, his muscles locking. He recognized the boy. He was from Group Ten, Eric's group. *This is it*, Frederick thought, and he cringed.

But the boy had paused, recognizing Frederick. He started to lower his arm.

Frederick's breath whooshed out in relief. The boy frowned. He drew his arm back again and hurled the ball. Frederick's eyes snapped shut. His hands flew up, palms out, to protect his nose from the blow . . . but it never came.

Frederick opened one eye and saw Nosebleed's back stretching like a wall between him and the boy from Eric's group. The ball was rolling away.

"Guess I'm out," Nosebleed said, turning to face Frederick. He was pinching his own nose, which had started bleeding. Whether it was because he'd gotten hit or it was one of his regular nosebleeds, Frederick didn't know. Nosebleed shrugged at Frederick good-naturedly and headed for the edge of the field where everyone who had gotten out was gathered to cheer and jeer at the boys still playing.

Frederick started moving again, more slowly, look-ing to see where the balls were. Ant Bite was close. He grabbed a ball and threw it, hitting another boy in the back so hard the kid fell to his knees.

Frederick jogged, arms pumping at his sides. He couldn't believe his luck that Nosebleed had run up at that exact moment. Or maybe . . . had Nose-bleed blocked the ball on purpose? Why would he do that?

He didn't have time to think about it.

As he ran and dodged, Frederick lost track of how

long they'd been playing. At some point, he began to notice that there was more space between the boys on the field. There were only about twenty of them left. And the sidelines were getting crowded with kids who were out.

Frederick hadn't been the first one to be knocked out. He hadn't even been *one* of the first ones out. He hadn't done so bad after all. Even if he got out right now, he had lasted a long time. His legs, which should've been aching with exhaustion, suddenly felt strong and fast.

He put his head down and jogged. Then someone was coming at Frederick with one of the balls, closing in. Frederick put on a burst of speed and leaned forward. He heard the ball hit the ground, and he ran harder. He was doing it! He was playing well. He was winning, and it felt good. It felt natural, like what Frederick was born to do. Like up to this point he'd been living a sham life, some other poor loser's identity that he'd had to put up with. And now, finally, he was living the way he was supposed to.

He made it to the end of the field and turned around. There were only five others still playing.

Most of them were at the far end of the field, and as he watched, a ball bounced off one of the boys, who shouted in frustration and then headed for the sidelines.

The kids who had been knocked out were yelling, shouting over one another. Frederick pushed his hair off his forehead, panting, and as he caught his breath, the shouts from the sidelines became clearer and stronger in his ears.

"Dash! Dash! Dash!" they shouted.

Frederick's heart pounded. They were cheering for him. The boys on the sidelines were chanting his name, clapping, jumping up and down.

While Frederick was listening, at the other end, two more boys got out. Besides Frederick, that left only two others, and they were scrambling for the balls, which were bouncing across the ground.

Frederick stood very still at his end of the field, hoping the other two wouldn't notice him down there.

Of course, it didn't help that the boys on the sidelines were shouting his name. But still, Frederick thought, the two boys would try to get each other out first.

They didn't. One of the boys grabbed a ball and turned and ran, ignoring the other boy entirely and heading right for Frederick.

It was Specs. And the other boy—who was tearing after him now—was Ant Bite. Both of them were clutching balls and coming toward Frederick.

Frederick was at the far edge of the field. He couldn't run away from them. But he couldn't just stand there either. He was going to have to run *at* them. There was nothing for it. He started running toward Specs. They were speeding at each other like two trains about to collide head-on. But as soon as Frederick was within throwing distance, he moved at a diagonal. Specs changed direction to intercept him.

Frederick dodged. Left, right. But Specs matched him, every move, getting closer and closer. Ant Bite was closing in on the pair of them. Then Specs was yelling and pulling back his arm. The ball left his fingertips.

Frederick yelled and ducked just as Ant Bite threw the ball in his own hands. Ant Bite's ball collided, midair, with Specs's. The balls ricocheted off each other. One arced in Frederick's direction.

The other ball rebounded and hit Ant Bite in the shoulder.

Frederick lunged forward and scooped up the ball that was rolling past him.

He was panting. His pulse throbbed in his ears. The ball that had hit Ant Bite was rolling away. Specs twisted toward it, moving to retrieve it, looking back over his shoulder as he did and squinting at Frederick.

Frederick had his ball in his hands. Specs was right in front of him. *Close.* Close enough that Frederick should be able to hit him.

But he remembered earlier, throwing the ball and it bouncing on the ground. He knew that if he threw and missed, Specs would have *two* balls. So Frederick did the only thing he could. He held the dodgeball out in front of him in both hands and ran after Specs.

It was like someone had muted the boys on the side. All he could hear was his breath and Specs's shoes hitting the ground. At the edge of his vision, he saw the boys on the side jumping up and down, their mouths moving but no noise coming out. In front of him, Specs's elbows pumped as he ran.

Frederick's legs picked up speed. Specs was right
in front of him. Then Frederick's toe caught on the
ground and he tripped. He fell forward, the ball in
his hands, no way to break his fall, and as he went
down, in slow motion, he saw the rubber ball just
barely . . . *boop* the back of Specs's calf. Specs let out

a surprised gasp. Then Frederick's chest hit the ground.

The volume turned back up.

"You're out!" Ant Bite yelled at Specs.

Eric's whistle sounded, and the campers roared, "DASH!"

14
Frederick, Victorious

"OKAY, OKAY!" ERIC SHOUTED OVER THE BOYS. "GAME over. Dash wins."

Frederick lay on the ground, the words sinking in. He had won. He had *won*!

"YEAHHH!" He jumped to his feet and punched the air. Then he spun around and pointed at Specs, who was slouching toward the edge of the field. "YES!" Frederick yelled. "Yes!"

The boys on the sideline were applauding and cheering. "Go, Dash!"

As he looked at the boys clapping for him, Frederick's whole body seemed to become lighter, like his tennis shoes might come off the ground. The pine trees around the field were tall and straight and greener than green. The sky stretched above. The boys' voices were as sharp and crisp as . . . as Doritos. Was this how it felt to not be a flea? Nothing was wrong, and everything was right, and Frederick wished he could freeze this moment in time and stay in it forever.

Then he spotted Nosebleed and the Professor. They were standing together at the edge of the field, a little removed from the other campers. They had their arms around each other and were cheering. Frederick could make out their voices through the roar.

"That's our boy!" they yelled. "Go, Dash!"

Specs stalked over to stand by them. Frederick picked up the dodgeball at his feet, tucked it under his arm, and started toward his group, too.

Then the Professor lifted his arm—the one that wasn't slung around Nosebleed—and, looking at Frederick, he beckoned. He waved him over in a universal gesture of true friendship, acceptance, and camaraderie.

The Professor shouted, "Come on, Dash!" and waved him over again.

Frederick's heart soared like a kite, rising high on a swell of wind.

Then Ant Bite stepped in front of him.

Frederick jerked to a stop.

"Now we *have* to go," Ant Bite said, glancing over his shoulder at Eric and the campers milling around on the sidelines. He pulled the small bag that he'd packed for Frederick off his shoulder and held it out.

Frederick's heart hung in the air a moment and then plummeted.

He hadn't forgotten about Ant Bite's and the others' plan to run away, but his victory at dodgeball had been so magnificent that it had made the others' plan seem no bigger than a gnat. And he had assumed the rest of Group Thirteen would feel the same way. But the bag was dangling from Ant Bite's hand.

The light dimmed. The trees looked scrubby and short. And Frederick's perfect moment was over, just like that.

"Quiet, campers!" Eric shouted. "We're going to the river for laps!"

The boys' hands paused mid-applause and dropped to their sides. They groaned and exchanged horrified looks with one another, forgetting all about Frederick and his victory.

"What about breakfast?" someone asked.

The boys were all talking at once, complaining about missing breakfast and asking why they weren't sticking to their schedules, and where were their own counselors?

"Did you carry that thing while you were playing?" Frederick asked, jutting his chin at the pack. He sidestepped until Ant Bite was no longer between him and the crowd of boys who were now dispersing.

Ant Bite grabbed Frederick's sleeve to pull him back, but Frederick jerked his arm away.

"Hey, stop walking!" Ant Bite said, stepping on Frederick's heel.

"*Aargh!*" Frederick yelled in pain, and stopped so suddenly that Ant Bite ran into him. "Leave me alone!" Frederick snapped, turning around. His neck was hot.

"*Whoa!*" Ant Bite said. "What's your problem?"

"What's *my* problem?" Frederick exclaimed. "What's my problem," he said again, in exasperation. He didn't know how to explain it. He didn't know how to say that he was tired of being a flea. And that he had just *almost* had what he'd always wanted, only he wasn't even going to get a chance to enjoy it.

What he did know was that he was suddenly very angry and upset, and Ant Bite was standing directly in the path of that anger.

"I never said I was actually going to go on a cruise with you. We were just talking last night. I can't— I can't believe you didn't realize that." He started to turn back to where the other guys from Thirteen were waiting. But before he'd taken two steps, Ant Bite was in front of him again, blocking his way.

"We helped you win," Ant Bite said in an accusing voice, and flung his arm out, indicating the dodgeball field. It was obvious what he meant. Since they'd helped Frederick win, he owed it to them to go along with their trip to Port Verde Shoals.

"You didn't help me win," Frederick said. Maybe Ant Bite and the others had done a little bit to help. Maybe they had helped a few times. But really, he had done a lot of it himself. He remembered running, dodging, weaving in and out. *He* had done that. Yeah, maybe he was a flea and all that, but he wasn't totally useless. And he was sick of everybody acting like he was. He pushed Ant Bite aside.

"What about what you said last night?" Ant Bite said. He scrambled to get in front of Frederick again, and he put his hands against Frederick's chest and gave him a shove. "About cruises being so great and how it was the one time you could get away from your problems."

"So what!" Frederick said, shoving Ant Bite in return and pushing past him.

He made it to the edge of the field, where Nosebleed and the Professor were waiting for them. They were the last ones left. Specs was a short distance away. He'd started back toward the cabin to change, but he was dragging his feet so much that he was still in earshot.

"Hey," Frederick started to say to Nosebleed and the Professor, but then something pushed him hard in the back. Frederick lurched forward, staggering into the Professor. He caught his balance and spun around to see Ant Bite standing with his hands curled into fists.

"No fighting!" Nosebleed pleaded.

Ant Bite's face was stony. "You were talking about how you got to go on vacation and get away from your problems. Well, I've got problems, too!"

"Then deal with them yourself!" Frederick said. "Everybody else does."

Nosebleed gasped. The Professor winced as if Frederick's words stung. Frederick clicked his teeth together. Specs had stopped walking and turned back to them.

Ant Bite stuck out his chin. "If we stay, we'll get in trouble," he said. "They're gonna find out that it was us who did the tires and the phone."

"And the window," Nosebleed added.

"And the—" the Professor began.

"So we *have* to go now!" Ant Bite said, urgency tingeing his voice.

"*I* didn't do any of that stuff!" Frederick said. "And I didn't tell *you* to!" He pushed his hands through his hair.

"Yes, you did," Ant Bite said. "We did this because of *you*. This was your idea. If we get in trouble, you do, too."

"I don't know why you're so upset," Frederick said nastily. "Somebody like you should be used to being in trouble."

The words *somebody like you* echoed in Frederick's head. He wasn't sure why, but he immediately knew that it was something he should not have said.

"I mean," Frederick said, trying to explain what

he'd meant, "what's the big deal? You're always kicking rocks at people, waving knives around. Aren't you in trouble all the time?"

The silence prickled Frederick's skin. But he was right, wasn't he? Ant Bite really *had* done all those things. Maybe Nosebleed and the Professor hadn't really deserved to be sent to a disciplinary camp, but Ant Bite had.

Ant Bite's jaw was tight. He looked at Frederick for a moment, and his chest heaved. Frederick was sure that Ant Bite was about to cry or yell or hit him, but then the other boy just shrugged, and his face went completely blank.

"Whatever," Ant Bite said. "Maybe you're too scared to go. Maybe you don't actually have any problems you have to get away from. But I'm going." He looped the strap of the bag over his shoulder. Then he turned and started walking across the dodgeball field, away from the river and the other campers and the buildings.

After a few steps, he stopped and looked over his shoulder, past Frederick, at Nosebleed and the Professor.

"Are you guys coming?" he asked in a rough voice.

"Well, I mean, if Dash isn't going . . ." The Professor trailed off uncertainly. "It was his idea. He's the one who knows about cruises."

"I *never* wanted to go," Nosebleed said.

Ant Bite's eyes cut to Specs.

Specs lifted his gaze to Frederick but didn't quite meet his eye.

Frederick remembered the catch in Specs's breath when the dodgeball hit him.

Specs shrugged slowly. "I'll do whatever Dash wants to do," he said.

Ant Bite looked at them all. Then he turned around again, straightened his shoulders, and kept walking.

Frederick watched him go, and he was sure that Ant Bite was just about to chicken out and turn around . . . come back. Of course he was.

But Ant Bite was getting farther and farther away. Frederick shifted his weight from foot to foot. He thought he ought to *do* something now. Maybe call Ant Bite back or run after him and apologize. Except Frederick didn't think he'd done anything wrong. Nothing he needed to apologize for.

He looked back at the others. The Professor and

Nosebleed were exchanging uncomfortable looks. Specs was watching Ant Bite leave with an expressionless face.

"Come on," Specs said dismissively. "He's just jealous he didn't win." He started back toward the camp, and Nosebleed and the Professor slowly turned and went with him.

"He'll come back," the Professor said to Frederick as he went. "He'll get scared and come back."

Frederick wasn't sure, though. Something about the way Ant Bite's face had gone blank like that bothered him.

The feeling he'd had before . . . the feeling of being a winner, something more than a flea . . . it was gone, but he could still remember the shape of it, like the smoke skeleton that hung in the sky after a firework's sparks had burned away. As that glorious feeling faded, Frederick came to a decision.

The right thing to do was to find an adult and tell them everything. Tell them about Ant Bite running off and about Frederick being lost. Frederick headed toward the buildings. He didn't want Nosebleed or the Professor to get in trouble. He didn't want Ant Bite to get in trouble either, even after all the stuff he'd done. But Frederick needed to get this straightened out once and for all. He was going to tell. Maybe he would leave out the part about the phone line, but that was it.

A roaring noise to his left made him look up. A truck was flying through the woods, bouncing over tree roots, coming right at him.

"*Aaah!*" Frederick yelled.

The truck's brakes screeched. The whole machine lurched forward and then jerked to a stop, the engine growling. Heat blew off the metal grille, stirring the hairs on Frederick's arm.

He stood frozen to the spot, nothing moving except his dancing arm hairs.

The engine cut off, and a woman with a short ponytail and a counselor's uniform sprang out of the truck cab and slammed the door so hard Frederick felt it in his teeth.

"What were you *thinking*?" the woman shouted as she marched up to him. Her hiking boots went *scrunch, scrunch* against the sandy earth. "Don't you know to look both ways before you step in front of a diesel truck?"

Frederick was still petrified, or he would have

been able to explain to the woman that he hadn't looked both ways because there was no *road* in between the cabins, so there was nothing to look both ways *for* except maybe a rogue deer or a bunny rabbit. Also, he had it on good authority that none of the trucks were working because someone had slashed their tires.

All of those would've been good things to tell the woman, but Frederick could only stare at her, with every muscle in his body clenched.

"How have you even survived this long?!" the woman yelled. "Hey! Answer me, kid." She adjusted her name tag with a sharp yank. It said *Gloria Harris, Counselor. Piedmont State, Forestry Management.*

Up ahead, Specs, Nosebleed, and the Professor had turned around and were watching the scene with wide eyes. Some of the other campers had run out of their cabins when they'd heard the brakes squeal. Benjamin was jogging toward the truck, a walkie-talkie in each hand. Then a pale boy with pointy eyebrows got out of the passenger side of the truck.

"Dash, are you okay?" Benjamin called as he hurried toward Frederick.

"*Urgh,*" Frederick groaned in answer.

At the exact same time, the pale boy sneered at Benjamin and said, "Why do *you* care?"

"Glo, you nearly killed Dash." Benjamin stopped beside Frederick and wiped the sweat off his forehead with the back of his hand. "Why were you driving so fast?"

"*Dash?*" Glo looked from Benjamin to Frederick. Then she pointed at the pale boy who'd gotten out of the truck. "*This* is Dash."

15

The Real Dash Blackwood

"YOUR NAME'S DASH, TOO?" FREDERICK ASKED, staring at the new boy.

The boy shook his blond hair out of his eyes. "I'm *Dashiell Blackwood*," he corrected Frederick. He said his name like it was in italics, and the implication was obvious. Someone who was so special that he had to italicize his name, even when he was talking, someone like *Dashiell Blackwood*, was not to be spoken to, looked at, or breathed on by someone like Frederick.

"Oh," Frederick said, realizing that this was *the* Dash. And he shouldn't have been surprised that the real Dash Blackwood had shown up, but he was.

The thing was, he had gotten so used to being Dashiell Blackwood that he now felt like Dashiell Blackwood kind of belonged to him. It was like he'd found a stray dog and taken care of him for a while and gotten attached. He didn't want to give Dash back to this boy with the sharp eyebrows.

"But"—Benjamin pointed at Frederick with one of the walkie-talkies—"this is . . ."

The Professor, Nosebleed, and Specs were easing closer. Frederick was beginning to think that it would be better if this conversation took place in private, but Benjamin was already going on.

He indicated Frederick again. "*He's* Dashiell Blackwood."

"*This* is Dash," the woman called Glo insisted, jabbing a finger at the new boy. "I picked him up at a police station in St. Mary's." She paused and then said, with something close to respect, "He robbed a bakery with a curling iron and a tabby cat."

Dash—the real Dash—sighed and looked around the camp with a sour twist to his mouth, like he wasn't impressed by what he saw.

"So," Benjamin said. "So . . . there are two Dashiells?"

"*Noooo.*" Glo's eyes closed, and her fingers curled into fists, like she was trying to stop herself from strangling Benjamin. She opened her eyes and pointed at the pale boy. "This is Dash." Then she turned to face Frederick.

He took a step back.

"Who are you?" Glo demanded.

"I'm . . . *uh* . . ." Frederick glanced at the boys from Group Thirteen and then looked back at Glo, who was staring at him without blinking. He didn't know what else to say, so he told her the truth. "I'm Frederick Frederickson."

Behind Frederick, Nosebleed made a surprised *puh* sound.

"There," Glo said, snapping her fingers. "That's Frederick." She pointed at Frederick. "And this is Dash." She pointed at the new boy. "Now we all know our names, and . . ." She raised her eyes heavenward. "*Why* am I even having this conversation?" She snapped her eyes back to Benjamin. "I need to talk to Eric, like, yesterday. Where is he?" She looked this way and that, as if expecting Eric to materialize from behind a tree.

A few of the gathered campers pointed toward the river, and Glo turned in that direction.

"This is Dashiell Blackwood." Benjamin was shaking his head and frowning at Frederick in consternation. "I registered him myself."

Frederick opened his mouth with the intention of saying something that would make everything clear, but he realized he didn't know what that would be.

"You know what?" Glo said. "You figure this out, 'kay? Write me a report when you do."

She started to stomp off but stopped midstride, one hiking boot up in the air. She tipped her chin back and raised one finger. "There *is* . . . ," she said slowly, lowering her boot to the ground. "There *is* an alert out for a missing boy." She pulled a phone from the pocket of her khaki shorts and started tapping away at it. "I just got it this morning . . ."

"I'm not a *missing* boy," Frederick protested, glancing at Nosebleed, the Professor, and Specs.

Missing boy sounded like he was some little kid who'd wandered off at the park and gotten lost. Frederick was ten, for crying out loud! He wasn't missing. He was just here. At camp. Hanging out. He was just hanging out at camp like cool ten-year-olds did.

"Are you supposed to be here?" Glo asked, not looking up from her phone.

"Okay, so I was having a fight with my friend Joel," he began.

"*Urgh!*" Glo yelled. She gripped her phone hard and lifted it over her head like she was about to throw it across the camp. Then she took a breath and calmly slid it into her pocket. She looked up and saw Frederick, Benjamin, Dashiell, Nosebleed, the Professor, and Specs staring at her.

"No service." She flicked a strand of hair out of her face. "So what's your name again?" she asked. She was looking at Frederick now with *interested* annoyance, instead of just annoyed annoyance.

"Frederick Frederickson," he said.

She blinked.

"I know," Frederick said. "It sounds made up."

"No, no," she said, shaking her head. "I remember the name on the alert being something stupid like that."

She clapped her hands together. "Okay. Here's what we're going to do. Dash"—she pointed at the pale boy—"go to the food tent and tell them I said you could have a late breakfast. Do *not* run away, steal anything, or get within ten feet of anything resembling a Cabbage Patch Kid. Benjamin, come with me to find Eric. You—lost boy," she said, looking at Frederick, "you come, too." She spun on her heel and headed for the main building.

"*We* didn't get breakfast!" a boy called after Glo. "How come Dash gets breakfast?"

She didn't answer the boy, and she didn't look back to see if Frederick and Benjamin were following her. They weren't.

"You're not Dash?" Specs said. "I knew you weren't," he added immediately. "I knew something was off about you."

Nosebleed was standing with his hands hanging at his sides, looking at Frederick with hurt eyes.

"So you lied to us," the Professor said.

"No!" Frederick said. "I didn't lie."

The three boys stared at him.

"I didn't lie to *you*," Frederick said. "I lied to Benjamin." He turned to see Benjamin's stricken face. "And I'm sorry!" he said. "I didn't . . . I didn't mean to lie to anybody. It was an accident. Ac-ci-dent." He sounded out each syllable and tried to smile.

The others didn't laugh.

"How can you *accidentally* tell a lie?" the

· 193 ·

Professor asked. His voice wasn't accusing. It was calm and steady like always, and for some reason that was worse.

"Umm . . ." Frederick remembered staggering out of the boat and smelling the pancakes. He remembered Benjamin holding out Dashiell's name tag and the feeling that he was meant to be at Camp Omigoshee. "A lot of things happened," he began.

"So, let me get this straight," said Specs. "Once upon a time, a lot of things happened and then you lied. The end." He started walking toward their cabin. "That's a great story," he called over his shoulder. "You should write a book."

The Professor turned away, too.

"We're going swimming," Specs said.

"Wait," Frederick said, hurrying after them.

"You don't come," Specs ordered, turning and holding up a hand, stopping Frederick. "You're not supposed to be here."

Frederick looked at Nosebleed.

"Nosebleed," Frederick said, "I didn't mean to hurt anybody's feelings."

Nosebleed took a deep breath. Then he turned away, too.

Frederick watched them walk away, and even though he was standing on solid ground, it felt like he was falling from the bell pull all over again.

Benjamin sighed. "We should go with Glo," he said. "We need Eric to sort this out."

Frederick ignored him. He took a few steps after Group Thirteen. "Come on, you guys. I'm literally the same person I was before," he yelled. "And you liked me then."

As the words came out of his mouth, he realized they were true. They had liked him. They hadn't been mad when he'd been the one to lose them the rope-climbing relay. Not really. They had dragged him back to camp last night. They had wanted to go on a cruise with him. They . . . they had helped him win at dodgeball. Except for Specs, and Frederick knew that that was just Specs being Specs.

And Frederick understood what a fantastic thing it was, having people like you.

"I tried," he pleaded after their retreating backs. "I tried to tell you my name was Frederick, but you didn't believe me!"

They didn't look back.

After a moment, Frederick turned and followed

Benjamin toward the main building. The soles of his tennis shoes scuffed the ground with every step. His red jersey swished around his legs. When he got to the flagpole, he turned back to see if he could make out any of the boys from Thirteen. He couldn't. They were gone.

"What do you mean there's sand in the fuel tanks?" Glo was demanding when Frederick walked into Eric's cabin.

She and Eric faced off across the desk, both of them on their feet. Benjamin was standing with his back pressed against the wall, looking like a life-size statue of a camp counselor.

"I *mean*," Eric said, "they didn't just slash the tires. They put sand in the gas tanks, too."

Frederick sank into a cracked leather chair beside the door, waiting for whatever they were going to do with him. He looked at the broken window beside the desk. Someone had Scotch-taped a manila folder over the shattered pane.

"These boys have never known discipline," Eric went on. "This is what happens when we don't teach young people discipline and character. And discipline!" He reached up and pulled off his sunglasses.

Frederick recoiled. Seeing Eric without his glasses seemed profoundly *wrong*, like seeing a snail without its shell. The counselor's eyes were small and watery, and the skin usually covered by his sunglasses was pasty white against his tan face. Eric snatched a Kleenex out of a box on the desk and started polishing the lenses as he marched toward the door.

"Wait right there!" Glo said, and Eric stopped as suddenly as if she'd yanked an invisible leash.

"Hurricane Hernando's turned," Glo said.

"Of course it has," Frederick muttered to no one in particular. He slouched in the chair and tipped his head back until it rested against the wall.

"That's why I was breaking my neck to get here," Glo said, ignoring Frederick. "I tried to call the camp, but I couldn't get through. The storm's headed right for us." She took a step back and tucked flyaway hairs behind her ears. Her eyes went wide, and she let out a breath, seeming to deflate, as if the seriousness of the situation had just hit her.

But Eric flicked his hand as if to say *pish* to Hurricane Hernando. "It's just some wind and rain," he said. "People of character—"

"That's right, Eric," Glo said, rolling her eyes. "Our good *character* will save us from the eighty-five-mile-an-hour wind."

"It's not that bad." Eric drew himself up and put his sunglasses back on. "They're exaggerating."

"They?" Glo said. She put her fists on her hips. "Who's *they*?"

Eric opened his mouth to answer, but Glo didn't let him get a word in.

"Maybe *they* is the Jacksonville Zoo, which is evacuating all its animals." Glo's voice rose as she took a step toward Eric. "Or maybe—maybe *they* is the entire state of Florida, which has closed."

"I think—" Eric started.

Glo's eyes bulged. "Maybe *they* are the people at the Syfy Channel, who just bought the film rights to the disaster movie that is about to happen to us!" She sucked in a breath and then let it out slowly. She removed a nonexistent speck from her shirt. "And you have *sand*," she said primly, "in your tanks."

The counselors fell silent, all of them probably contemplating the fact that a Category Five hurricane was on its way to ravage Camp Omigoshee, and they had only one working diesel truck with which to evacuate seventy-four not-yet-transformed boys and one liar who nobody liked.

Frederick lifted his eyes to the ceiling. Someone had stuck a smiley-face sticker against one of the ceiling panels. "Bring it on," he said.

16

The Rock

"ARE YOU READY TO GO?" GLO WAS ASKING FREDERICK
ten minutes later.

She, Benjamin, and Frederick stood outside Eric's
cabin. The counselors had decided that Glo, three
other counselors, and Frederick were going to
squeeze into her truck and drive to the nearest
town. Glo would take Frederick to the police station
and hand him over to them so they could contact
his family. Then she was going to find three school
buses ("I'll steal them if I have to") that didn't have
sand in their tanks or gashes in their tires and
have the counselors drive them back to camp, load
up the boys, and drive west like *The Fast and the*

Furious . . . only in school buses instead of sports cars.

"*Mmmm* . . ." Frederick looked around camp. Obviously he didn't want to be in the camp when the hurricane hit, but he felt like he wasn't done here. He at least needed to say good-bye to the guys in his group. The morning was sunny, and a light breeze was beginning to stir. It didn't look like there was a hurricane coming.

"We're hitting the road in less than five minutes." Glo started walking off in the direction of a counselor who was crossing the camp. "So you'd better pack up and have your stuff in that truck"—she pointed at the big truck that she'd almost run Frederick over with—"in less than three."

"Less than three," Frederick repeated blankly.

"*Minutes.*" Glo's eyes bugged out. "Three *minutes.*"

"Okay," Frederick said, trying to think of what stuff he needed to get to take home.

Mr. Mincey's boat was down by the river under the willow tree where Frederick had left it. Maybe he could come back and show Mr. Mincey where it was. Ant Bite had taken his bag of lost-and-found stuff, so he couldn't pack that. The only other thing he had was his dirty shirt he'd swapped for the red jersey. He'd left the shirt on the floor by his bed.

"Ant Bite!" Frederick exclaimed, realizing. He spun around to Benjamin, who was standing at his shoulder, looking lost. "Benjamin, Ant Bite's gone. He went away before Glo got here."

"Went away where?" Benjamin asked.

"I don't know!" Frederick said. "I mean, maybe . . . he might've . . . He might think that he's going on a cruise," he said. Was Ant Bite really trying to go to Port Verde Shoals? Or had he just run away for a little while? Frederick didn't know.

"*Okay*," Benjamin said. He hitched up his shorts. "A cruise," he said, disbelief bleeding into his voice.

"The point is he's gone!" Frederick said.

"Don't worry," Benjamin said. "We'll find Ant Bite and evacuate him, too."

"He was really mad," Frederick pressed, trying to make Benjamin understand the seriousness of the situation. "And he doesn't know about the hurricane."

"Dash, relax." Benjamin put a hand on Frederick's shoulder. "Me and the other counselors are trained professionals."

Frederick didn't correct Benjamin about using the wrong name. Instead, he looked at Benjamin—really looked at him. His earnest, disappointed face. His neat counselor's uniform and gigantic shorts. His name tag, which had twirled around to face backward again, showing the number thirteen. Benjamin gave Frederick a reassuring smile.

Then a bird flew over and a watery green turd landed on the shoulder of Benjamin's blue polo. It slid down the fabric, and all of Frederick's hope for saving Ant Bite seemed to slide with it.

"Oh my g—"

"Goodness gracious," Benjamin said, twisting his head and pulling on the sleeve of his shirt so he could inspect the bird poop.

Frederick grabbed the top of his head and looked around, trying to come up with an idea for what to do. Then he spotted Specs, Nosebleed, and the Professor walking out of Group Thirteen's cabin in their swim trunks.

"I'll be right back," Frederick said to Benjamin, and he ran over to the boys.

He stopped right in front of them. The Professor stepped around him and kept walking.

"Wait," Frederick said, reaching for the Professor's arm just as Specs grabbed the front of his jersey and shoved him back several steps.

"Get out of our camp." Specs's nose was an inch from Frederick's.

"There's a hurricane," Frederick said, cringing back from Specs's breath and prying the other boy's fingers off his shirt.

"Get out of our camp," Specs said again. "You don't belong here. You're not a part of our group, understand?" He stepped sideways so that he was between Frederick and Nosebleed and the Professor, like he was *protecting* them from having to come face-to-face with Frederick. That was ridiculous. Frederick wasn't dangerous. He was one of them.

"Come on," the Professor said to Specs. "Let's go swimming."

"There's a hurricane!" Frederick said. "It's called Hernando, and it's coming this way, and it's so bad the Syfy Channel's going to make a movie about it."

Specs didn't back down. "I haven't heard of any hurricane," he said.

"That's because you're so self-involved you don't

care about the world around you," Frederick said automatically.

Specs looked startled for a second, like he was trying to figure out what Frederick meant; then his nostrils flared.

"You get out of here," Specs said, tilting his head back so he could squint down his nose at Frederick. "'Cause the next time I see you, I'm going to snap your glasses."

"I don't wear glasses," Frederick said.

Specs lifted a finger, backing away. "Exactly," he said, and turned around.

The Professor shrugged at Frederick and then followed Specs.

"I just wish you hadn't lied to us," Nosebleed said.

"I didn't mean to lie!" Frederick said. "And I'm worried about Ant Bite."

Nosebleed started for the river, his plasticky swim trunks *shrush-shrushing* as he walked.

Frederick kicked the ground in frustration. "Ant Bite's in trouble! There's a *hurricane!*" he yelled as they walked away from him. He realized it was the second time that morning he'd found himself shouting at their backs.

"All campers report to the main building for an emergency meeting!" a counselor shouted into the megaphone. "All campers report to the main building!"

"See!" Frederick said, calling after them. "See?"

Specs and the others stopped and exchanged looks. The Professor glanced back at Frederick. Then all three of them turned and headed toward the main building, stepping wide around Frederick as they went.

"What about Ant Bite?" he called.

This wasn't right. This wasn't fair. It wasn't like Frederick was asking them to do anything unreasonable. He wasn't asking them to forgive him or to be friends with him again. He was asking them to help him figure out how to save Ant Bite, who was supposed to still be their friend.

This wasn't Frederick's job. It wasn't his responsibility. This wasn't even a job he could do. This was a job for somebody like the Rock or something. Not Frederick. Only, the Rock wasn't coming. And sure, there was a whole spectrum of people who were between the almighty Rock and Frederick the Flea. But none of those people were going to help.

Frederick walked around in a tight circle, winding himself up. "Fine," he said to himself. "Fine. It's all fine." He stopped walking in circles and started toward the field where they'd played dodgeball, in the direction Ant Bite had gone in earlier. "I'll just go get Ant Bite."

"Dash!" Benjamin yelled. "Where are you going?"

"Tell Glo I'm coming!" Frederick shouted over his shoulder, starting to run. "I'll be right back!"

17

The Kudu

"DASH, COME BACK!" BENJAMIN'S VOICE CALLED AFTER him. "Dash!"

Frederick ran past the small cabins at the edge of the camp and didn't slow down when he got to the dodgeball field. His feet pounded across the scrubby grass. Less than an hour ago, on this field, he had experienced glory for the first—and maybe last—time. But he didn't have time to think about that right now. He raced over the far edge of the field and into the forest that surrounded Camp Omigoshee.

Frederick turned his head this way and that, looking for Ant Bite, trying to spot a flash of white T-shirt or a glimpse of dark hair against all the brown and green. Ant Bite couldn't have gotten too far. He had been walking, whereas Frederick was running, so Frederick was bound to catch him soon.

He would find Ant Bite and warn him about the hurricane. Ant Bite would probably still be mad at him, but Frederick would just have to live with that. They would come back to camp together and be okay. That was all that mattered.

There were no paths through the woods, but Frederick's feet seemed to instinctively find a route by avoiding the thickest brambles and tightest clusters of scrub.

But when the brambles and scrub got thicker and thicker, Frederick slowed to a walk, panting. The giant red jersey stuck to his sweaty back like Saran Wrap to a pudding.

"Ant Bite!" Frederick called.

He stopped walking so that the crunch of leaves under his shoes cut off. Frederick listened so hard he felt like his ears were twitching. The chirps, peeps, and squawks of dozens of birds grew louder and louder as he listened. The roar of wind in the pine tops, the buzz of insects. But no answering call from Ant Bite.

Frederick cupped his hands around his mouth and tipped his head back. "Ant Bite!"

The birds went on with their own conversations, as if Frederick, shouting down below them, didn't matter.

He started walking again, swatting at a gnat that was flying around his head.

A tree root caught the toe of Frederick's shoe, and he had to hop several steps to keep his balance. He regained his footing and steadied himself, looking back at the dumb root that had tripped him. When he looked up again, something had changed. The woods seemed different . . . less friendly.

What if Ant Bite hadn't come this way? He might've gone a little more that way, Frederick thought, looking to the left. Or a little more *that* way. He looked right. Or maybe he'd gotten farther than Frederick had guessed. He might be a mile ahead of Frederick.

How much time did he have before the counselors left without him? Slowly, Frederick looked back in the direction of the camp.

The trees that he had walked past stretched strangely into the distance, like a camera zooming out. Everything looked different from this angle. Was camp really that way?

Frederick needed to go back. He needed to go back before he *couldn't* find his way back. But without wanting to, he remembered how Ant Bite had helped him win at dodgeball and everything he'd said after, and Frederick winced. *Somebody like you . . .* The words echoed in his mind.

The gnat that had been orbiting his head was now trying to drink the fluid off the surface of his eye.

"Argh!" he growled at the empty woods, and slapped at the gnat.

He turned back around and stomped after Ant Bite again. Or . . . at least, he started stomping in the direction he *hoped* Ant Bite had gone.

"Ant Bite!" he yelled, and he heard a creaky, squeaky note in his voice. He clenched and un-clenched his hands as he walked. His foot crunched a pinecone.

Rough pine bark was everywhere he turned. Frustration and fear made his vision shaky, and his breath was so loud in his own ears that he worried if Ant Bite did call out to him, he wouldn't be able to hear it.

Crunch, crunch, crunch went the leaves. *Whoosh-whish* went Frederick's breath. After a while, he began to imagine that he heard voices, wheedling their way through the noise in his own head. *Great,* he thought, *I'm hearing voices now.*

Frederick slowed down. He *did* hear voices.

"Ant Bite?" he said, and he picked up his pace, jogging toward the sound.

As the voices got louder, the trees began to thin, and suddenly, Frederick jogged out of the forest and found himself at the bottom of a ditch on a roadside. The blacktop was high, over his head, and a steep bank of grass rose between him and the pavement. He'd never realized, riding in the car, how tall highways could be compared to the land around them.

He heard banging and then a man's voice called out, "Make sure those bolts are secure!"

Relief flooded Frederick. They were adult voices. They could help him. Maybe they'd even seen Ant Bite! He climbed up the hill and onto the highway and looked left and right.

Frederick did a double take.

To the right, far off, several tractor-trailer trucks were wrecked, lying on their sides, having skidded off the road and into the trees. "*Whoa*," Frederick whispered. He moved closer.

Tires were suspended in the air. Metal cabs were crushed like Coke cans. Glass frosted the road, glittering in the sun.

It looked like something out of a movie . . . well, Frederick amended, a movie like *Transformers*. Not one like *The Secret Garden* or *Winnie the Pooh*.

He moved cautiously toward the trucks.

"Is anybody hurt?" a woman yelled.

"We're all good here!" a man answered.

As Frederick got closer, he saw men and women moving around the trucks, climbing up on the overturned trailers, and calling out to one another. None of them had noticed Frederick yet.

He paused, trying to take in the scene. A logo on one of the trucks said JACKSONVILLE ZOO AND GARDENS. Glo had said the Jacksonville Zoo was evacuating, Frederick remembered.

He was about to call out to them when an explosion of squawks from one of the trailers made him jump. The squawks died down, and then rose again. It sounded like an entire flock of birds was trying to get out of the trailer.

"There are nails in the road!" a man shouted. He tore the baseball cap off his head and scraped a heavy work boot against the asphalt. "Someone's put nails in the road!" He slapped his baseball cap against the side of his thigh.

"Hey!" a woman shouted. "He's out! The male's gone!"

The man swore and tugged his cap securely back on his head.

"Get the tranq!" the woman called.

"Okay, everybody listen up," the man shouted. "We've got to get him back! Mitch! You got the tracker?"

"Yeah!" a man shouted.

Frederick lifted a hand, opening his mouth.

"This way!" Mitch said.

"Hey!" Frederick called.

The men and women jogged down the road, away from Frederick.

"Wait!" he called, running after them. They were shouting to one another, and maybe they didn't hear him, or maybe they thought he was one of them, running and shouting. Whatever the reason, they didn't slow down.

"Wait!" Frederick yelled again, his feet pounding the pavement. He ran after them until his lungs burned. Then he kept walking down the middle of the road, watching the zookeepers get smaller and smaller until, when they were far ahead, they turned off the road and disappeared into the woods. And Frederick was alone again. He walked along the empty road.

On either side of the road, pine trees tossed in the wind. The trunks swayed. Clouds grew thick in the sky. Frederick was trying not to notice these things. Instead, he was trying to think about how hurricanes were slow moving. His traitorous brain reminded him that he'd once thought the Omigoshee River was slow moving. He tried to think about how the hurricane was probably way out in the ocean, so he had plenty of time. He tried to think that he was going to find Ant Bite really soon. He tried to think about how any minute now he would hear the growl of the diesel truck and how Glo's eyes would bug out as she yelled at him for running off. He tried to think about how hungry he was. This last one was easy because he hadn't eaten anything all day, and he would've, for real, given away his entire college savings account for some of Miss Betty's pancakes right then.

Frederick walked to the edge of the road and half climbed, half slid down the ditch. He went to the first tree he came to and sat down, leaning back against the rough trunk. The wind lifted the hair off his forehead.

The chances of someone in a search party finding him . . . in time . . . were probably, like, one in a hundred thousand. He imagined Raj's voice saying, *It wouldn't be an even number like that. It would probably be, like, one in three hundred eighty-two thousand and five.*

"Shoot," Frederick muttered, banging the back of his head against the pine trunk.

His eyes watered, and so what? Nobody would know. He might as well cry.

But what if, a voice in his head insisted, someone from the search party walked up at the exact moment he was crying? He would wipe his eyes as fast as he could, but it would be obvious that he'd *been* crying because his eyes would be puffy and red. They would know. And he would know that they knew.

He pushed himself off the ground and started to walk off the crying feeling.

As he walked, it did seem like he was leaving his tears behind, but every step brought him closer and closer to the fact that he had been wrong. He had been wrong at the dodgeball game and after the dodgeball game, too. The others had helped him win, and he hadn't said thank you. Ant Bite and Specs and the Professor had wanted to go on a cruise, and he hadn't even listened to them. He'd been mean to Ant Bite. He'd been a bad person.

He'd known that for a while now. He'd known it even before he left camp to go after Ant Bite. He'd been trying to *not* know it, because every time he thought about it, shame squeezed his heart.

The fact was that he had acted like Joel and Raj. Maybe even worse. He'd acted the way he'd always hated. He hadn't meant to. Not exactly. It'd just happened. But he knew that that didn't make it all right.

Frederick was going to have to find a way to fix it. He would fix it, and then he would feel better, and he would never do it again. He just hoped he *could* fix it.

"God?" Frederick said out loud. "I know that last time this didn't work, but maybe that's because you were saving up because you knew that I'd need an even bigger favor later. That was really great of you." Frederick wanted God to know that he didn't have any hard feelings about the whole not-helping-him-when-he-was-in-the-river thing. "But I was just hoping that . . . if you don't mind too much . . . you could maybe get me out of here?" He paused. "And Ant Bite, too," he added. "And soon. Soon would be good. I mean, whenever you want is fine, and help me to make it right with Ant Bite and the others, okay? Okay, I'll be ready to get out of here in five, four, three . . . two . . ." Frederick swallowed. "One."

There was nothing. No sound of a person coming to help him. No sign of Ant Bite. Frederick was alone.

Then the wind shifted the clouds, and the sky brightened. A column of sunlight lanced through the gloom. Frederick's eyes, drawn to the sunbeam, followed it down, and there, standing in front of him, framed by brilliant light, was a strange and graceful animal. It reminded Frederick of a deer. It had a dusty-colored coat with white stripes. Its horns were tall and spiraled gently upward. The animal held its head proudly. Its ears flicked, and it turned its neck to regard Frederick with startled, wet eyes.

"Wow," Frederick breathed. The deer must've been the animal that had escaped from the truck, the one all the zookeepers were looking for.

Frederick didn't move for fear of scaring the animal away. The ears flicked again, and its tongue stretched out and touched its nose. Other than these tiny, sudden movements, it stood perfectly still while all around it the woods tossed and swayed in the wind. Frederick had the sense that he and the deer were in a bubble and that inside it, time had stopped. He could live in this moment forever, and nothing could touch him. He didn't need to feel ashamed of anything or afraid of anything.

Then there was motion behind the deer. Frederick looked and saw an enormous lion placing its front paw soundlessly on the ground. Its golden eyes were fixed on the deer.

Frederick gasped just as the lion unfurled like silk and launched itself at the beautiful animal. The deer made a sudden bleating sound as the lion's jaws closed on its hindquarters. The deer's front legs scrabbled at the ground like it was trying to run even as the lion dragged it back.

Frederick's mouth opened to scream, but his lungs were deflated, and the only sound that came out was a weak *eeeee*, like air leaking from a tire.

Then someone was running out of the woods toward him. Frederick *eeee*-ed with more energy.

"Run!" Ant Bite yelled, dragging at Frederick's arm. "Run!"

Frederick didn't need telling twice. Well, Ant Bite had just told him twice, so he *had* needed telling twice. But he didn't need telling a third time.

He ran, pumping his arms, keeping pace with Ant Bite, and he would've left Ant Bite in the dust if he could've, but the smaller boy was running flat-out, too.

"That's a li— a li—" Frederick choked out as he ran.

"I know it's a lion!" Ant Bite yelled. "Run!"

18
The Letter

FREDERICK RAN. ANT BITE WAS BESIDE HIM. THE brambles and the tree roots and the scrubby bushes didn't matter anymore. Frederick flew through and over every obstacle in his path.

Sweat poured off his face. His chest burned, and in the spaces between his heartbeats, he imagined teeth closing on his ankle and jerking him backward.

Pain stabbed through Frederick's ribs, and he staggered. He grabbed a tree to keep himself on his feet and looked over his shoulder, thinking he'd been attacked, before he realized the woods were empty behind him. It was just a stitch.

"Come on. Come on," Ant Bite panted. He had pulled up a few feet ahead of Frederick. He was clutching his knees, breathing hard. He leaned forward and spit and wiped the back of his hand across his mouth. "Come on," he said again.

Frederick nodded, pushed himself off the tree, and followed Ant Bite.

They staggered through the woods in what Frederick hoped was the direction of camp.

"It was a boy lion," Ant Bite said after a few minutes.

Frederick blinked. Had it been a boy lion? Did it matter? He didn't think it mattered.

"It had a mane." Ant Bite patted both sides of his neck, where the lion's mane had been. Then he settled his hands back onto the strap of the shoulder bag slung diagonally across his body.

Frederick didn't say anything.

"It's good I saw you," Ant Bite said in a remarkably calm voice for someone who'd just seen a full-grown lion killing a beautiful animal. "I saved your life."

Again, Frederick said nothing. He was grateful that Ant Bite had run up when he had. But he didn't trust himself to open his mouth to say thanks, just in case that *eee* sound came out again. He guessed that seeing a lion attack made people react differently, because Ant Bite kept up a stream of commentary.

He told Frederick about weird trees he'd seen on his way to the road. He told him he hadn't been scared to be in the woods alone, but he'd gotten bored without anyone to talk to. He told Frederick about how he'd planned to make it to Interstate 95 and hitch rides from drivers heading south. And how he was excited to go on a cruise, even if he was by himself.

"I only decided to come back when the weather started getting scary." Ant Bite looked up at the heavy sky and the trees bending in the wind. As he spoke, a pinecone dropped between the two of them, making Frederick jump.

"This looks pretty bad," Ant Bite said.

When Frederick finally spoke, his voice was raspy and strange. "It's a hurricane. There's a hurricane coming," he said. "Glo told us just after you left."

Ant Bite looked at him. "Like a *hurricane* hurricane?"

Frederick nodded.

"*Huh*," Ant Bite said.

"I came out here to warn you," Frederick said, and then he stopped himself from saying any more. He didn't want to upset Ant Bite by telling him they were lost in the woods and everyone else had been making plans to leave a couple of *hours* ago.

"Thanks," Ant Bite said. "Thanks for coming out here to warn me."

"You're welcome," Frederick said in a strangely formal way.

They were both quiet for a moment.

"Who's Glo?" Ant Bite asked.

"She's a counselor at camp. She showed up right after you left. Oh." Frederick remembered. "I . . . *uh* . . . I've got to tell you something." He shifted his shoulders. "Glo brought the real Dash Blackwood to camp. I'm not Dash. I was just pretending to be Dash because . . . because I wanted to stay at camp. But my name is Frederick Frederickson." He paused to take a breath and realized how bizarre all of that sounded.

"I know," Ant Bite said.

"What I mean is—" Frederick began. "Wait. You do?"

"Yeah," Ant Bite said. "I mean, I didn't know you

were Frederick Whoever, but I knew you weren't Dash."

"How?" Frederick asked.

"Because I've met the real Dash before." Ant Bite kept his eyes on the path ahead, stepping high over fallen limbs. "We went to the same school before he got expelled for trying to run over kindergarteners with the floor polisher."

"Oh," Frederick said.

They walked in silence for a moment.

"It's a Category Five," Frederick blurted. "The hurricane that's going to hit is a Category Five. That's the biggest category there is."

"*Whoa*," Ant Bite said.

Frederick nodded. "Glo says it's so bad they're going to make a movie. Like a disaster movie, and everyone else is evacuating. They even evacuated the Jacksonville Zoo, which is why . . . the lion." He bobbed his head.

Frederick expected Ant Bite to be shaken by this news, but the younger boy just held on to the bag's strap and let out a small "Wow."

Ant Bite didn't seem too worried about the hurricane. Now that the lion was far behind them, he was walking steadily through the woods, like this was a nature hike. Watching him step over tree roots and kick pinecones out of the path made Frederick feel less anxious about the whole thing.

"Why didn't you tell the others?" he asked. "About me pretending to be Dash?"

Ant Bite shrugged. "I figured it was your business. So your name is . . ." Ant Bite raised his eyebrows at Frederick.

"Frederick Frederickson." He paused. "My mom named me. She said she wanted me to have a name people will remember."

"A name people will remember," Ant Bite repeated. "That was nice of her to think about that."

Frederick had never heard anyone describe his mom as nice before.

"She is," he said. "She's nice."

Frederick was hot and tired, and the red jersey smelled . . . weird. Like a stranger's funky bad sweat. He pushed his hair off his forehead and blinked, looking ahead of them. A sliver of green roof showed through the trees.

"Hey!" He reached out and tapped Ant Bite's arm.

"What?" Ant Bite looked up.

Frederick pointed at the green roof.

"That's . . ." Ant Bite's voice was faint.

"Camp!" Frederick said with relief.

He and Ant Bite walked faster. As they got closer, the buildings appeared out of the trees like something out of a fairy tale.

They made it to camp and walked between the buildings on the narrow paths packed by hundreds of feet.

Every so often the climbing bells clanged in a gust of wind. The flag snapped in front of the main building. Other than that, the camp was silent. Frederick hadn't realized how much noise the campers made until they were gone.

He and Ant Bite didn't speak. They didn't need to. They were thinking the same thing. No truck was here . . . at least not one with tires that rolled. No phone was here. Not one that worked. No other human was here. What *was* here was the two of them. Camp Omigoshee was deserted.

"What's that?" Ant Bite pointed toward the main building.

Something white flapped from one of the double doors. Frederick and Ant Bite exchanged a look and ran over.

They found a letter taped to the door.

Dear ~~Dash~~ Frederick and/or Ant Bite,
If you are reading this, then you've made it
back to camp.

"Yep," said Ant Bite with a nod.

Don't leave! Stay in the main building! We're
out looking for you, and if we find you, we'll
come right back. And if we don't find you,
we'll be back before nightfall. (Probably
around eight or nine?) I don't know when
nightfall is exactly and I can't look it up on
my phone because there's no service. So we'll
be back sometime soon!

Sincerely,
Benjamin Merkel
P.S. Eric says nightfall is at nineteen
hundred hours!
P. P. S. Glo says she'll talk to the police and
have them call your families.

Frederick sagged with relief. He looked at Ant Bite and saw the other boy's face mirroring his own exhausted happiness.

Finally, they were done with all the running and being lost and being attacked. All they had to do was wait for Benjamin and the search party to come and get them. They were saved.

19

Tim Howard

FREDERICK AND ANT BITE WAITED ON THE FRONT PORCH of the main building. They sat against the wall with their knees up, watching the flag whip in the wind and keeping their eyes peeled for any sign of Benjamin and the search party.

The wind picked up even more, the trees swaying farther and farther, and a drizzle of rain blurred the camp beyond the edge of the covered porch. Neither Ant Bite nor Frederick pointed out these facts. They also didn't mention that the sky was getting heavy.

All the things they weren't saying crawled over Frederick's skin, until finally, Ant Bite broke the silence.

"We should find a snack," he suggested.

"Yeah," Frederick said, quickly pushing himself to his feet, wondering why he hadn't thought of a snack.

A snack was a quick meal that they could fix and take with them to enjoy in the truck or car if Benjamin showed up before they'd eaten it.

In fact, Frederick decided, following Ant Bite into the dark belly of the main building, he was sure that if they made a snack, Benjamin and the search party would show up soon after. It was like something he and Ant Bite had to do in order to summon help.

Once inside, Frederick patted the wall by the door, finding the light switch. Fluorescent lights flickered to life across the ceiling. The main building was a big, open room with linoleum floors and round tables. Half the chairs were turned upside down on the tables, as though somebody had been in the middle of cleaning the floor when they had to evacuate. A swinging metal door at the back of the room led to a long, narrow kitchen, which Frederick and Ant Bite searched for food.

In the refrigerator they found jugs of milk and enormous plastic bags of shredded cheese. The pantry had towers of cans: baked beans, tomato sauce, Vienna sausages. Frederick pulled down a can of beans and a can of sausages. Next, he and Ant Bite started opening drawers, searching for a can opener.

"Jackpot," Ant Bite said. He was standing on a counter and looking into an open cabinet.

"You found it?" Frederick asked.

"No," Ant Bite said. "I found something better. I'll teach you how to make my specialty."

Frederick looked over Ant Bite's shoulder at several boxes of cereal.

Ant Bite's specialty was a sandwich that consisted of two pieces of white bread smeared with pancake syrup and French's mustard. And in the middle was Honey Bunches of Oats cereal.

The bread was soft, and the cereal was crunchy, and when Frederick pressed it down, it squished and then crunched. He bit into it. It tasted sweet and vinegary at the same time.

"'S'not bad." Frederick took another bite.

"*Mmmumph,*" Ant Bite agreed.

They had taken their snack into the main room, choosing a table close to the front doors so they wouldn't miss Benjamin and the search party coming in.

After three sandwiches, Frederick was feeling pretty content, all things considered, and he decided it was time he did something he'd been putting off.

"Hey. This morning when I told you I didn't want to go on a cruise, it wasn't anything personal. And I'm sorry . . ." Frederick didn't look at Ant Bite as he spoke. Instead, he talked to a mounted trout hanging on the wall. "I'm sorry," he tried again, "that I told you to deal with your own problems. That was pretty mean."

"Nah, you were right," Ant Bite said.

"No, I wasn't," Frederick said.

"You were," Ant Bite insisted. "Everybody's got to deal with their own problems. That's just the way it is."

"No, it's not," Frederick said. "Friends—I mean, people should help each other out."

Ant Bite shrugged. He looked uncomfortable.

"And I'm sorry I said you were in trouble all the time. I didn't mean it." Frederick knew now that he'd been wrong about the guys in Thirteen. He'd assumed that everybody who was at a disciplinary camp must be a bad person, but they weren't all bad. Ant Bite was really brave. And Nosebleed was kind. The Professor was tough. And Specs was . . . Specs. And Frederick wasn't as *good* as he'd thought he was, either.

"It's fine," Ant Bite said, shrugging again.

The trout's tail was bent like it would swim away if it weren't stuck to the wall.

"Why *did* you get sent here?" Frederick asked, realizing that he didn't know. "You said you had problems."

"Just forget about it," Ant Bite said, not looking at Frederick. "It's nothing."

"Come on," Frederick said. He wanted to help. Whatever Ant Bite's problem was, Frederick was sure they could find a way to fix it. And maybe that would help him make it up to Ant Bite for the way he'd acted before.

"I said *no*." Ant Bite jerked, and his arm bumped

his plate, nearly knocking it off the table. "You can't help me anyway."

"Why don't you just tell me what's bothering you?" Frederick asked, leaning back and holding his hands up.

"Because it's not a big deal," Ant Bite said. "Really."

"Come on," Frederick said again. "It's—"

"Okay!" Ant Bite said, leaping to his feet. "If I tell you, will you lay off?"

"All right." Frederick lowered his hands slowly, waiting for Ant Bite to settle down.

Ant Bite sank back into his chair and didn't speak for a moment. When he did, he said, "So when I was in third grade, we had to do this science project."

"Okay," Frederick said.

"I made a robot," Ant Bite said.

"Wow." Frederick had never made a robot. He didn't know anyone else who'd made a robot. For the science projects at *his* school they made baking soda volcanoes or grew bean sprouts in plastic bags.

"Yeah. It was good, too," Ant Bite said. "I spent a

long time on it. I glued some of those googly eyes on it. I named him Tim Howard."

Frederick wondered how he'd come up with that name. Did the robot just look like a Tim Howard? Did he know someone named Tim Howard?

"But this other kid," Ant Bite went on. "Rich. We were the first ones at school that day, and we were the only two people in the classroom. I don't know where Mrs. Paulson had gone. But Rich took Tim Howard off my desk and wouldn't give him back. When the other kids came in, Rich said that Tim was his and that *I* was the one who was trying to take him."

Ant Bite dragged his finger through the puddle of syrup on his plate.

"What'd you do?" Frederick asked.

"I told the teacher," Ant Bite said, like it was obvious.

"Oh," Frederick said. "Right."

"But she didn't believe me," Ant Bite said. "She liked Rich better. His mom was one of the class parents, and she was always helping out with field trips and stuff. So that day Mrs. Paulson told everybody that Tim Howard was Rich's science project. And everybody was telling Rich he did a good job and not to listen to me. He even said he had come up with a name for it . . . *Kevin*."

The trout's bottom lip was open in shock.

"What'd you do then?" Frederick asked.

"I broke him." Ant Bite gazed blankly at the syrup on his finger.

"*Rich*," Frederick said.

"No," Ant Bite said, rolling his eyes. "Tim Howard. I was angry, and I broke him. I was really upset about it. I mean, I should've just let Rich keep him. That would've been better for Tim."

"Did you get in trouble?" Frederick asked.

Ant Bite shrugged. "Kind of. I mean, my teacher got on to me right then and told me I couldn't go to recess. But later, my parents called and they even came to the school and said that it was *my* robot. They said they'd seen me working on it. But Rich's parents came and said the same thing. They said it was *his* robot."

The trout's one visible eye was wide with alarm.

"His parents *lied*?" Frederick couldn't believe somebody's parents would lie about them making a robot. That seemed like a really big thing to lie about. Not a little lie like, *Oh, I'm sure he studied for his test* or *Of course my son enjoys your class.* It seemed like you shouldn't be able to lie about whether your kid had built a robot.

Ant Bite nodded. He licked the syrup off his finger. "My teacher said the only fair thing to do was to not punish anybody and not give me *or* Rich a grade for the project."

"How's that fair?" Frederick asked. "That's not fair."

Ant Bite shrugged. "The thing is, I could tell my teacher believed Rich and his parents. I could tell she thought I'd lied. Or she wanted to think that I'd lied. Before all that happened, I was really smart. Like, I was as smart as the Professor.

"But then after this one thing, which I didn't even do, it was like everybody forgot that I was a smart, good kid, and all they thought about me was that I'd broken Rich's robot. That was when I started doing bad things. I figured, everybody already thinks I'm bad, so why should I try to be good? After that, I wouldn't do my homework. Or when we were supposed to be quiet, I would talk. Or during break I'd go just outside the bounds we were supposed to stay in."

The wind howled over the roof.

"Is that why you were sent to camp?" Frederick asked. "For doing all that stuff?"

Ant Bite sighed. "I've never done anything really, *really* bad. Not like Dashiell. The real Dashiell. But when I started fourth grade this year, my new teacher had a special meeting with my mom and dad, and she said that I should go to this camp. She was really nice about it. She said it would be like a reset, and when I got back I could start over. But I don't know." He shrugged.

Frederick waited for more, but Ant Bite was done.

"So . . . can you help with that?" Ant Bite looked up at him.

Frederick leaned back in his seat. He'd gotten interested in Ant Bite's story and forgotten that the reason he was listening was to figure out how to help.

"Why don't you just . . ." Frederick's voice trailed off. "Well, why don't you just *quit* being bad?"

Ant Bite was quiet for a moment. "I don't know if I can," he explained. "I started doing all this stuff. And then I started doing more of it . . . I don't know if I can stop now. Even if I go back to doing what I'm supposed to, all the other kids are still gonna keep treating me like a bad person. So why even bother, you know?" He took a breath. "And why'd everybody believe Rich instead of me? That's just not fair."

The trout seemed to be looking at Frederick, waiting to hear his answer.

"*Uhhh.* My friends have this theory of life," Frederick began. "They say that everybody has a place in the world, like there's a natural order.

"Some people are lions. There's this guy at my school named Devin and he's a lion. And some people are gazelles. And some people are meerkats. And I'm a flea."

Frederick didn't know exactly why he thought this story would be comforting to Ant Bite, but he kept going anyway.

"I thought I could change the fact that I'm a flea," Frederick admitted. "I thought if I could do something right or if I could win something, then I'd be as good as Devin and then . . ." He wasn't going to tell Ant Bite about how he wanted a best friend who would hang out with him. He wasn't going to admit he was *that* pathetic. "I thought everything would be great."

"So," Ant Bite said. "What happened?"

"*Ummm* . . . well, I nearly got eaten by a lion," Frederick admitted ruefully.

"Oh," said Ant Bite.

The small windows set high in the wall were dark, and rain drummed against the roof.

Something was bothering Frederick. The story he'd just told Ant Bite . . . *his* story had sounded wrong in his ears. It hadn't sounded true. He knew that it *had* been true. But it had been true for an earlier version of himself. Now, he realized that he didn't care so much about being a flea or not being a flea. Becoming *that* guy didn't matter as much as he'd thought it had. He just wanted to fix everything he'd messed up.

"Is that it?" Ant Bite asked, looking over at Frederick. "Is that the advice?"

Frederick shrugged.

"That wasn't even advice," Ant Bite protested.

"Give me a break," Frederick said. "I'm trying."

Ant Bite shook his head. "This is just about the *worst* help anybody ever got."

"I was trying to let you know I understand!" Frederick said.

"*I'm a flea and everybody else is a lion*," Ant Bite said in a gloomy voice like Eeyore the donkey.

"That's not the way I said it," Frederick protested. "But okay, fine, I get it. Anyway, I don't think you're as bad a person as you're making out. I mean, you saved me from that lion—the real lion. A bad person wouldn't have done that."

"It was adrenaline," Ant Bite said with a grin. "If I'd stopped to think about it, I probably would've let it eat you."

"*Nuh-uh*," Frederick said. "You wouldn't have—"

"Nah, I'm just kidding, man." He smiled. "And I don't care if you're a flea or what. I'll still be your friend."

At Ant Bite's words it was as though a ball of light began to glow inside Frederick's chest, warm and bright. He snuffed it out immediately.

Probably, when Ant Bite said *friend*, he didn't mean friend. When he said *friend*, he probably meant person-whom-I-do-not-hate. Or maybe he was just saying *friend* to be polite. Although Ant Bite had never seemed particularly concerned about manners.

But Ant Bite couldn't really mean he and Frederick were friends after everything Frederick had done. Could he?

"Listen—" Frederick began.

There was a cracking sound from outside, followed by a tremendous *pow!* Frederick and Ant Bite yelled just as the lights in the main building blinked out.

20

The Water Is Lava

WITHOUT ELECTRICITY, THE MAIN BUILDING WAS pitch-black. Frederick waved his hand in front of his face and saw nothing. He heard Ant Bite unzipping the bag and digging through its contents. Then the emergency flashlight clicked on. The two of them carefully walked out onto the front porch. Rain fell at an angle, hitting their faces even though they were under the roof. Outside, there was just enough light to see by, but the sky had turned an ugly bruise color. Benjamin's letter, still taped to the door, was smeared and soft from the water.

"There," Frederick said.

The wind was roaring in the treetops. A limb had broken out of a tree and knocked a big metal piece off the electric pole. A tangled wire was on the ground beside the building.

"Don't touch it," Ant Bite said in a voice tight with fear.

Frederick didn't intend to.

"I think," Ant Bite said, "I think that's the transformer."

They went back into the building and closed the doors.

"Benjamin's letter said they'd be here before dark," Ant Bite said, acknowledging their counselor's absence for the first time. "It's dark now. I wonder where they are."

"They're probably almost here," Frederick said. "And they better apologize for being late."

"Yeah," said Ant Bite. "I bet they're telling each other now, 'I hope Ant Bite and Frederick aren't too worried.'"

Without discussing it, they both went back to the table where they'd eaten their sandwiches. Instead of sitting in the chairs, though, they sat cross-legged on the floor. They scooted under the table and listened to the rain getting heavier and heavier as the minutes passed.

Earlier that afternoon, while Frederick and Ant Bite had been sitting on the porch waiting for Benjamin, it hadn't really been raining. It had been misting. Then, while they were eating their sandwiches, it had started drizzling. When the limb had taken out the electricity, it had been raining. After another hour or so, it was just getting ridiculous.

The rain was coming in horizontally and hitting one entire wall of the main building like bullets.

Of course, Frederick had never heard bullets hitting a building in real life, but he was sure that it would sound like this. He thought that Ant Bite must be thinking the same thing, because he kept turning the flashlight on and pointing it around the room through all the table legs. Frederick thought he was checking to see if there were little holes in the walls where the rain had punched through.

Ant Bite turned off the light, muttering, "Don't want to kill the batteries."

What felt like thirty seconds later, he turned it back on to scan the room again. Frederick was about to tell Ant Bite to cut it out and give him the flashlight when Ant Bite yelled, "Hey, what's that?" and crawled out from under the table.

Frederick hurried after him, banging the top of his head. He was rubbing his skull as he walked toward the spot where Ant Bite stood, pointing the light down at the floor.

"What's . . ." Frederick's voice trailed off.

Water had rolled under the double doors and was spreading across the smooth floor.

Obviously, it wasn't good to have water in the building. The water was supposed to stay outside. But on the bright side, Frederick thought, it was just water. Water would just get them wet; it wouldn't hurt them. He turned to Ant Bite, about to say something to that effect, but Ant Bite was backing away from the puddle like it was lava.

"We're going to drown," Ant Bite said, looking at the oozing line.

"No, we're not," Frederick said, thinking this was a major overreaction. "It's, like, a centimeter of water." He stepped into the shallow puddle to demonstrate how he was completely unharmed. He was just standing on some wet linoleum. It didn't even come up over the soles of his shoes.

"Yeah, but it's going to keep coming and fill the whole room." Ant Bite's voice was panicky.

"It's not going to fill the whole room," Frederick said. "That would be impossible.

"Listen," he continued in a reasonable voice when Ant Bite was quiet for too long. "When the water gets to here"—he grabbed the barrel of the flashlight in Ant Bite's hand and pointed the beam at a black scuff mark on the floor, a spot that was almost in the middle of the room—"*that's* when we'll need to worry." He had to speak loudly to be heard over the bullet rain and the wind.

"Okay?" Frederick said.

Ant Bite didn't answer.

"When the water gets up to here," Frederick said, and made a line with his finger on the wall, "*then* we'll need to be worried."

It was late. Just after midnight, according to the clock on the wall. The wind and rain had died down a bit, Frederick thought, but the water level continued to inch up. An ankle-deep layer of water now covered the entire floor and was rising slowly.

For the last several hours he had kept revising his estimate of when they would need to worry. *When it gets to this Band-Aid stuck on the floor, that's when we're in trouble. When it gets to the other wall, THEN we'll have a problem.*

Now, he sloshed back to where Ant Bite sat on top of a table. The other boy had gotten quieter and quieter until finally he was completely silent, and whenever Frederick turned on the flashlight to check the water level, Ant Bite stared at him with big eyes and didn't even remind him about the danger of killing the batteries. Frederick was starting to get freaked out—more by Ant Bite's silence than by the water. Ant Bite hadn't been scared of anything. Not rope climbing, not Eric, not Specs, not the idea of breaking into Eric's cabin or even running away from camp. But now he was scared.

Frederick pushed himself up on the table and let his legs swing down, the toes of his shoes touching the water. A *boom* came from somewhere outside. Limbs had been falling all night. Maybe even trees.

"We have to *do* something," Ant Bite said suddenly. He snatched up the flashlight Frederick had set down and hopped off the table.

The howling of the wind changed pitch then, and the building shuddered.

"What do you suggest?" Frederick asked, spreading his hands to indicate the flooded room, the lack of electricity, the lack of adults and trucks, the lack of telephones and can openers.

"We have to get out of here," Ant Bite said in a determined voice.

"Benjamin's letter said to stay in the main building," Frederick reminded him.

"Benjamin could be dead!" Ant Bite said, and started toward the front doors.

"Benjamin's not dead!" Of course he wasn't dead! Because that was impossible, because . . . Frederick thought of Benjamin, bouncing up to the food tent, a lanyard swinging from his fist. He thought of him looming over Frederick as he lay on the ground after falling from the bell. He thought of the counselor pulling at his own sleeve to observe the bird poo that had landed on him. "This is a hurricane! You can't go outside during a hurricane." Frederick waded through the darkness, following Ant Bite and the skittering light in his hand, trying to reach him before—

Ant Bite opened one of the doors, and the wind got ten times louder and gusted into the main room, hitting Frederick so hard that it knocked him back a step.

"Close the door!" Frederick said, grabbing the edge of the door with both hands and trying to force it shut.

But Ant Bite stepped into the opening between the inside and the outside.

"We have to stay inside!" Frederick yelled.

"What's that?" Ant Bite yelled over the wind. He was holding the flashlight in both hands.

"I don't see anything!" Frederick said. He didn't. Everything was dark and wet and wet and dark outside. But as he continued to look, he did see the weak light flashing off something white. It was small and hard to make out, but Frederick slowly realized what he was looking at.

A hundred feet in the distance, wedged between some pine trees, was Mr. Mincey's boat. The boat had been down at the river, Frederick knew. He grabbed the barrel of the light in Ant Bite's hands and moved it over the camp and realized that the river was *everywhere*. It had risen and spread into the woods. The boat must have floated up and gotten stuck in the trees.

"That's my friend—my friend Joel's boat," Frederick said. "Well, it's his dad's boat."

"We should go get in it!" Ant Bite said. He pulled the light away from Frederick and pointed it back at the streak of white in the darkness. "A boat would float no matter how high the water got."

Frederick was shaking his head. Everywhere the light touched, wind was whipping water into froth. The roof shuddered over their heads.

"*No*," he said to Ant Bite. "That's too dangerous. Limbs could fall on us. Like the transformer fell. *We* could fall out of the boat."

"We'll drown if we stay here!" Ant Bite shouted.

"No, we won't," Frederick said. "We'll—we'll stay on the tables, and if the water gets higher than the tables—which probably won't happen—then we'll go outside and get on the roof."

"How will we get on the roof?" Ant Bite demanded.

"We'll swim," Frederick said. "Or we'll find something that floats."

"I can't swim," Ant Bite said.

"You can't swim," Frederick said back to him,

not understanding. Then he remembered Ant Bite wearing the life vest when the campers did their swimming rotation. "Oh, brother," he muttered.

It was a serious problem, but it seemed so ridiculous to Frederick. And so annoying. He knew he wasn't being rational, but really, how could Ant Bite be so unprepared? It was like he had shown up for a cinnamon-roll-eating contest and announced that he was allergic to cinnamon. They were in the middle of a hurricane! With water everywhere! Being able to swim would've been really useful!

"Okay." Frederick tried to think of what they ought to do. He hadn't seen any life vests in the pantry. Maybe he could teach Ant Bite to float.

"We need to get in the boat," Ant Bite said before Frederick could come up with anything. He gripped the door frame and rocked back and forth on his feet, like he was getting ready to throw himself off a diving board. "Before the water gets any higher."

"No!" Frederick said. Every nerve in his body was screaming at him to go back inside and wait for Benjamin and the search party.

"I'm not staying here!" Ant Bite said. He looked toward Frederick.

Frederick couldn't make out his face in the darkness. Then Ant Bite started down the stairs of the porch, stepping deeper into the water.

Frederick held on to the door, indecision tearing him in two. Ant Bite was already disappearing into the darkness. If Frederick was going to go with him, he needed to leave right now. He didn't move. He couldn't. It was a terrible idea to go out in the storm. He had to stay inside, where at least he had a roof over his head.

But when he looked back at the dark and empty main room, Frederick didn't feel safe there. He felt alone. It seemed like no matter what he did, he always ended up alone. Falling branches hit the roof, making him flinch. Frederick realized he had made a mistake.

He didn't want to be alone. If you were with somebody else—if you had a friend—then even if terrible things were happening, at least there was somebody there to make you feel braver. It was hard to be brave by yourself.

"Hey!"

Frederick spun around. The flashlight beam arced across the porch as Ant Bite grabbed the doorway. He'd come back. "Listen," he said to Frederick. "I'm not leaving without you."

Frederick's heart unclenched.

"But I really think we need to go!" Ant Bite went on.

The light that Frederick had felt in his chest earlier was back again. This time he didn't try to stop it. He took a deep breath.

"Hey!" Ant Bite waved his fingers in front of Frederick's face. "Are you okay?"

Frederick shook his head, bringing himself back to where he was—the open doorway of the main cabin, his hair dripping rainwater in his eyes, and the hurricane raging around him.

"Yeah!" he answered. "I'm great! Let's go!" Frederick realized he was beaming. He could feel the grin on his face, and he knew that that was probably not the most appropriate reaction to have in the middle of a natural disaster, but he couldn't help it because it felt so good to have Ant Bite back. Even though he'd only been gone for about twenty seconds.

"*Uh* . . ." Ant Bite was looking at him with raised eyebrows. He didn't seem to share Frederick's sudden happiness.

Frederick laughed at Ant Bite's confused expression and stepped to the edge of the porch, calling over his shoulder, "It's just a little wind! We'll be fine!"

21

Teeth of the Storm

FREDERICK WADED FORWARD, HIS ARM LINKED WITH Ant Bite's. About four seconds after they had gotten off the front porch, the happy, glowy feeling in his chest had been replaced by a please-don't-let-me-die feeling.

The two boys bowed their heads together and hunched their shoulders against the wind. The water rose up to Frederick's knees, and even higher on Ant Bite. A current pulled at Frederick's legs, and the wind blasted against him. He put his foot down, and the ground seemed to fall away from him. He staggered, barely staying upright. With the next step, he staggered again. The water was getting deeper. Through his panic and fear, he slowly realized what this meant.

They were going downhill. Downhill was not good in a flood. He was about to shout a warning, but he felt a tug as Ant Bite's arm unhooked from his. Then Ant Bite was falling.

Frederick yelled and grabbed. The only part of Ant Bite he could reach was his face. Teeth closed hard on one of Frederick's fingers.

"Aaah!" Frederick shouted. The wind carried his yell into the night. He had a grip on one ear and Ant Bite's jaw, and he dragged Ant Bite up by these handles.

Ant Bite got his feet under him. He pushed Frederick's hand away from his mouth, grabbing Frederick's arm to steady himself.

The flashlight, which Ant Bite had been holding, was gone.

"You're okay!" Frederick said.

Rain ran down his face. He held on to Ant Bite and thought about bending down to see if he could find the flashlight. It must be on the ground nearby. The current wouldn't have carried it too far. Then he heard a sound.

He looked around. A dark shape seemed to be sweeping through the woods between them and the main building. Frederick didn't—

Boom. A swell of water reached Frederick's armpits. The ground shook, and shock waves rippled through Frederick's body like he was a giant tuning fork.

He reached out one shaking hand, and his fingertips brushed across papery bark. One of the towering pine trees had fallen, landing six inches from where Frederick and Ant Bite were huddled.

Boom. The sound came from farther away. Then again. *Boom.* Trees were falling all around them.

For a moment, Frederick was frozen. Then he grabbed a fistful of Ant Bite's T-shirt. "Run!" he shouted over the storm. "Run! Run! Run!"

They ran, holding on to each other's arms, pushing through the water, dragging each other forward.

They reached the boat faster than should've been possible. The boat dipped and scraped against the trees as Ant Bite reached up, gripped the edge of the hull, and then scrambled up and over.

Frederick held on to the edge of the boat. He couldn't climb as well as Ant Bite. The side of the boat was a vertical wall that was slick with water, and the wind was trying to tear him away from it. He pulled himself up but fell back at once, his arms giving out.

Frederick adjusted his feet. If he could just get a good jump off the ground. Or if he had something to climb up on.

"Come on!" Ant Bite yelled. "Don't let go!"

Both of these were things Frederick had already thought of.

He braced his foot against one of the trees the boat was caught in and pushed off. He got almost high enough to see into the boat, and then he fell back into the water. Frederick shouted in frustration. His heart hammered.

Ant Bite leaned back to balance the boat and gripped Frederick's arms, yelling through his teeth.

Frederick heaved himself up with all his strength.

Ant Bite's hands scrabbled frantically, pulling the back of the jersey. Then he grabbed the belt loop on the back of Frederick's shorts and yanked, hauling Frederick up with more strength than he could possibly possess in his thin arms. Frederick inched up the side of the boat, and his shorts inched up his backside.

"Okay, stop!" Frederick yelled. "STOP!"

But Ant Bite didn't stop. He kept pulling on Frederick's shorts, until Frederick splashed into the boat, panting and shaking.

He gasped in relief, but that feeling lasted only a second.

In his scramble to get in the boat, Frederick had dislodged it from where it was wedged in the trees. Now the wind was pushing them across the water, sending them ricocheting off tree trunks. Each crash jarred Frederick's body. He clung to the seat to brace himself.

"The boat's full of water!" Ant Bite yelled.

It was true. Frederick hadn't noticed it immediately because he was so soaked that it almost didn't matter, but he was kneeling in the bottom of the boat, in a pool of water.

He turned his face to Ant Bite, not able to see his expression in the dark. "That's because it's raining in it!" he yelled. And it was obvious to him, *now*, that this would be a problem.

Frederick looked down at the water around his legs.

"Scoop!" Ant Bite yelled. "Scoop! Scoop!" And he

cupped his hands together and flung water out of the boat.

For a moment, Frederick didn't move. With a sinking feeling he watched Ant Bite working against the rain, splashing water out of the runaway boat. Then he frantically started scooping water with his hands and flinging it over the side.

22
The Stupid Ending

EVENTUALLY, FREDERICK AND ANT BITE WERE TOO exhausted to do anything but hold on to the sides of the boat as the wind knocked them into trees and hurled sticks and leaves and water at them. Pine needles stung Frederick's arms and face as they hit him.

Gradually the rain stopped. The wind became a breeze and then a breath and then stilled completely as early light stained the forest around them.

Frederick had been wrong before about a little water not being too bad. After being wet for so long, he was shivering and shriveled. He and Ant Bite balanced on the boat's metal bench seats and propped their feet on the sides to keep them out of the water. The pinky finger on Frederick's right hand was bloody and aching from where Ant Bite had bitten it.

As the sun rose, they saw that they were floating through a world of water. It stretched in every direction. Everywhere, trees had fallen to the ground or snapped in half. Giant limbs speared the earth and rose out of the water. Their boat was dented and had deep scratches in the hull. It looked like it had been attacked by a pack of velociraptors.

"Isn't it a beautiful day?" Ant Bite said, smiling upward and closing his eyes against the sunlight. He looked like he'd been run through a washing machine, but he seemed cheerful. As if in agreement, a bird over their heads began to chirp.

"That was," Frederick said, "the worst idea anyone ever had. Ever."

"I'm sorry about your finger," Ant Bite said. "I didn't know it was your finger, and I thought I was drowning, and I just . . ." He clicked his teeth. "Hey, is that a monkey?" Ant Bite asked suddenly.

Frederick followed Ant Bite's gaze. A monkey was standing on a lower limb of a nearby tree, pulling on

its bottom lip as if it was perplexed at finding itself in a magnolia.

"It must be from the zoo," Frederick said. "I wonder how many animals they lost? One of the drivers said there were nails in the road."

Ant Bite's eyes widened. "*I* didn't put nails in the road."

"I didn't say you did," Frederick said.

"The Professor might've," Ant Bite said. "But I didn't."

"What?" Frederick asked. "Why would—"

"Do you hear that?" Ant Bite asked.

At first, Frederick thought Ant Bite was trying to distract him, but then he heard it, too. There was a growling sound, and it was growing louder.

"That's a motor," Frederick said.

A few seconds later, he saw Glo's diesel truck inching through the trees, angling toward them.

Eric was leaning out the passenger window with a pair of binoculars, surveying the woods.

"Hey!" Frederick yelled. He stood up, waving his arms. The boat wobbled dangerously, and he sat down again before he fell.

Eric's binoculars swept past the boat.

"Over here!" Ant Bite yelled.

"Eric!" Frederick shouted.

The binoculars swept back and stopped on them.

"Yes!" Ant Bite and Frederick cheered together.

Eric lowered the binoculars and pointed at them.

"Dash! Anthony!" Eric shouted in a raspy voice.

"Stay right there!" As if Frederick and Ant Bite were about to run away.

Frederick saw that Benjamin was behind the steering wheel. Through the windshield, he saw the counselor's face light up when he spotted them. He started punching the horn.

Beep, beep, beep!

Benjamin leaped out of the truck before it had come to a complete stop and ran over, splashing water as he came. Eric jumped out and strode toward the boat, too. The head counselor's socks sagged and bagged around his ankles. His sunglasses dangled from a strap around his neck.

"Are you okay?" Benjamin yelled over the splashing. "Are you hurt?"

"We're fine!" Frederick called back.

Benjamin reached them and leaned over, bracing his hands against his knees.

"You said you'd be here last night!" Frederick exclaimed, looking up at Benjamin from his seat in the boat. "Where were you?"

"Yeah, what happened?" Ant Bite demanded. "We got back to camp early in the afternoon. We waited in the main building forever and you never came!"

"We've been looking for you all night!" Benjamin's

blue polo was rumpled. He had purple crescents under his eyes, and his cheeks were covered in patchy stubble. But he looked great to Frederick. "And then Eric got the truck stuck—"

"I did not!" Eric snapped, walking up. He crossed his arms and looked at Benjamin. "You were the navigator. You should've warned me about that bog."

Eric adjusted his shorts as he turned to survey the flooded woods.

Benjamin rolled his eyes upward and then looked back to the boys. "Y'all are in about three inches of water," he said, looking down at the water. "I'm surprised that boat'll even float. Why don't you just get out?"

Frederick and Ant Bite looked over the edge of the boat and down. Then they looked at each other. They scrambled out of the boat and onto the ground that they could've been walking on for the last several hours.

Ant Bite and Frederick got in the backseat of the truck, and Benjamin drove slowly through the woods, dodging fallen trees.

"Thanks for finding us," Frederick said.

"Yeah," Ant Bite agreed fervently.

Eric twisted around to face the two of them. "Men of character don't leave anyone behind," he said.

"Do you know if my parents are okay?" There was a thread of worry in Ant Bite's voice.

"Where do they live?" Eric asked.

"Macon."

"That's really far inland," the head counselor told him. "They're fine."

Ant Bite didn't look completely relieved.

"They'll be a lot better once they know you're safe," Benjamin said. He glanced at Ant Bite and Frederick in the rearview. "Glo wanted to stay and look for you, too," he assured them. "But she had to drive one of the buses with the campers." He paused. "I told her I'd find you. Even though they didn't cover natural disasters or search parties in our training."

"You did great, Counselor," Frederick said.

In the rearview, Frederick saw Benjamin smile.

They finally made it to the road, but it was covered with fallen trees, too, and it took them ten minutes to reach a sign that said YOU ARE LEAVING CAMP OMIGOSHEE, WHERE BOYS ARE TRANSFORMED.

They hadn't made it much farther when they saw a car that had stopped, blocked by a tree. The car was familiar to Frederick, and just as he was saying, "Hey, that's my—" his mom, his dad, and Sarah Anne scrambled out of the Corolla, leaving the doors wide open.

"Frederick!" his dad yelled as they clambered awkwardly over the tree and then ran to the truck.

Before Frederick knew it, they were opening his door and dragging him out and into their arms, not even letting his feet touch the ground. His mom was sobbing and holding his head. His dad was hugging his legs, and Sarah Anne had his middle.

"Why didn't you evacuate?" Frederick asked when they finally put him down.

"Because you were missing!" Sarah Anne said, and punched him in the arm.

"Did you think we would leave without our baby?" Mrs. Frederickson rubbed her nose. "And then we g-got," she hiccuped, "a call from the police that you were here."

"We wouldn't have left the *cat* behind in that storm," his dad said. "Much less our kid."

Eric, Benjamin, and Ant Bite had gotten out of the truck and were standing a short distance from the Fredericksons. Mr. Frederickson walked over and shook all of their hands, even Ant Bite's.

While they were standing there, another truck drove up and stopped behind the car. It was Joel's dad in his Super-Duty four-wheel drive. And Joel was in the front seat.

Frederick felt like he'd missed a step going down stairs. It seemed like it'd been weeks since he'd seen Joel. It startled him to realize that Joel looked the same as always. But he looked different, too. Frederick didn't know how both of those things could be true.

"You're all right!" Mr. Mincey bellowed as he jumped out of his truck. He ran over and pulled Frederick into a hug that squished his cheek against Mr. Mincey's chest. Mr. Mincey was wearing the same blue shorts and flip-flops he'd had on at Joel's party, and he had a scrubby beard on his jaw. "We headed this way as soon as we heard." His chest was heaving against Frederick's face. "I-I've been out looking for you ever since the party."

"I'm sorry I took your boat," Frederick said in a muffled voice. "And I'm sorry I lost your motor."

Joel had gotten out of his dad's truck and was

walking over slowly. He looked rumpled and tired and a little shy, which wasn't like Joel at all. He kept glancing at Frederick and then looking away, like he was afraid Frederick was going to yell at him.

"It's all my fault!" Mr. Mincey exclaimed, letting go of Frederick and wiping away tears that were streaming down his face.

Frederick glanced at his dad, expecting to exchange an uncomfortable look with him. But Mr. Frederickson was wiping his own eyes.

"I should've taught all you boys how to drive the boat," Mr. Mincey said to Frederick. "I'm going to . . . ," he said. "I'm going to make sure the next time you're in my boat you can drive it right. I'll make a captain out of you, son." Mr. Mincey scrubbed his nose.

After hours of sitting on a metal bench seat in a hurricane, Frederick didn't want to get back in Mr. Mincey's boat ever again, but he didn't say that. He was too tired to string words together.

Joel was still standing back, but he took a few steps forward. "Hey," he said to Frederick, still not meeting his eyes. "I'm glad you're okay."

"Yeah," Frederick said uncertainly. He wasn't sure why Joel was acting so weird. Normally, he would've been telling everyone loudly how Frederick was bound to get lost in a storm because he was a loser, and how if *he* had been lost in a storm, he wouldn't have been scared at all.

"It was a stupid joke," Joel blurted then, shaking his head. "That thing about giving you the boat and making fun of you because you missed your vacation. I didn't mean for anything bad to happen. I thought I was being funny."

Everybody was looking at Joel, and his shoulders hunched up toward his ears.

"It wasn't funny," Joel said. "I'm sorry."

Everyone's eyes turned to Frederick then.

For a moment, he didn't know what to say. Joel had been terrible, and a part of Frederick wanted to tell Joel that yeah, he'd been awful and Frederick was done with him. But then he thought about how he owed the other guys in Group Thirteen an apology and how he really hoped they would tell him that it didn't matter. He wished they were here right now and that they would tell him that they still liked him, that they were still his friends.

"It's okay," Frederick said. He paused. "You're my best friend," he added.

Joel lifted his head and finally met Frederick's eyes. He looked startled, his eyebrows climbing. But then a smile broke out over his face.

Frederick felt himself smile, too. Then he realized that his mom and dad and Sarah Anne and Mr. Mincey, Eric, Benjamin, and Ant Bite were all looking at him and Joel. His neck got hot, and he shifted his feet.

"This camp," Mr. Mincey said to Benjamin, breaking the silence. "Is it occupied now? Are there more kids missing? 'Cause I'm willing to keep searching."

Benjamin rocked up onto his toes and then back on his heels. "The other boys have been evacuated to Valdosta. We're going there now to help get them back to their homes. They should be all right."

"Of course they'll be all right!" Eric said, puffing out his chest. "Safety and preparation are the hallmarks of the program here."

"Then how did these two boys wind up alone in the middle of a hurricane?" Frederick's mom demanded, rounding on Eric, who took a step back.

Mr. Frederickson put a steadying hand on his wife's shoulder.

"We need to get going," Mr. Mincey said, eyeing Mrs. Frederickson warily. "It should've taken us an hour to get here, but it took three. Storm's blocked so many roads." He eyed the tree across the pavement in front of the Fredericksons' car. "I had to get my chain saw out twice."

Mrs. Frederickson glared at Eric a moment longer, then turned to Frederick. "Let's go home, baby," she said.

Sarah Anne was already walking back to their car. Frederick's legs were suddenly heavy. He wanted to go home and sleep for a week, but his brain was slowly putting things together and realizing that *he* was going home, but Ant Bite wasn't coming with him. He was going somewhere else. His own parents were waiting for him. And Nosebleed, and the Professor, and Specs. How long would it be before he could tell them he was sorry? Or . . . what if he never got to?

"Bye," Ant Bite said, taking a step toward Frederick. He looked like he was going to hug Frederick, but then he held out his hand.

Frederick had only known Ant Bite for two days, but they'd survived a hurricane together and a lion attack and atomic dodgeball and rope climbing, and he didn't know what to say, but he was sure that *good-bye* didn't cover it.

He shook Ant Bite's hand. The other boy squeezed his bitten finger, and he winced.

"I . . . ," he started to say. "Thank you for . . ."

"Hey," Ant Bite said. "It's Anthony."

"What?" Frederick said.

"My name's Anthony." Ant Bite shrugged. "And I want you to know—I like you better than the real Dash."

Frederick tried to smile. Joel walked up to him and threw his arm around Frederick's shoulders.

"Come on, man," he said, and walked with Frederick to the car.

Despite Frederick's protests that he was perfectly fine, his mom actually buckled him into his seat, like he was a toddler. The doors slammed.

Mr. Mincey steered his roaring truck around, and Frederick's dad drove behind him.

Frederick looked back through the rear windshield. Eric was stoically watching them leave, his arms crossed. Ant Bite and Benjamin waved, and then they were so far away that Frederick couldn't see their faces.

His last thought, before he fell asleep against the window, was that this was a stupid ending.

23

Four Months Later

OF COURSE, FREDERICK HAD BEEN WRONG, AND THAT day when he'd said good-bye to Ant Bite wasn't the end of anything for anybody.

The counselors at Camp Omigoshee went back to college. Benjamin was spending a semester in Australia studying marsupials. Glo was going to graduate in a couple of months, and in her free time she was training to compete on *American Ninja Warrior*. Eric had a part-time job making smoothies. Frederick imagined that he wore his sunglasses even while he was blending almond milk and protein powder.

The state had lots of people cleaning up the camp, and Frederick's dad told him it would probably be an even nicer camp when they were done with the re-furbishments.

Mr. Mincey had gone online and bought a wet suit and scuba equipment, and he'd dived into the Omigoshee like a large seal. He found his motor on the riverbed and attached a chain to it and dragged it back onto the shore. He didn't find the anchor, but he bought a new one at Bass Pro and taught Frederick how to securely tie a line to it and tie that line to the boat.

The people at the Jacksonville Zoo were probably the busiest of all. They had lots of scientists and volunteers helping them search for all the missing animals. Most of them were found and recaptured without a problem. According to the news, one macaw and one animal called a kudu, which was similar to a deer, were missing, but people said they still might turn up.

And Frederick was busy, too. With help from Sarah Anne, his mom and dad, Raj, and Joel, Frederick had started his own fund-raising campaign.

Four months after Hurricane Hernando flooded a hundred miles of coast and ruined the Fredericksons' yearly vacation, Frederick found himself, at long last, on a ship in the Caribbean. Music blared. The sun blazed overhead, and there wasn't a single cloud in the enormous blue sky.

Frederick padded across the hot deck on bare feet and stepped up to the bar, where Sarah Anne was perched on a stool, sipping Sprite through a straw and chatting at the bartender.

". . . of course, it looks good on college applications," Sarah Anne was saying, gesturing with her hand as she spoke. "But that's not why I do it. I do it because I want to be an active and productive member of society."

"Another strawberry daiquiri, please," Frederick told the bartender.

"The only downside," Sarah Anne went on, crossing her legs and swinging one sandaled foot, "is that now everyone acts like I'm the 'fund-raising girl.' Like that's all I do. And it's not. I don't want to be doing fund-raisers for the rest of my life. I want to be, like, a television host or an advice columnist, because I'm really great at fixing problems. Or maybe I should be a lawyer. Or maybe an actress."

Frederick took the drink the bartender slid him.

He shifted the paper umbrella out of the way and caught the straw in his mouth as he walked back to his lounge chair.

"Hey, Frederick!" Nosebleed called from across the pool. He waved him over to where he and several other boys were having a cannonball contest.

Frederick lifted his drink at Nosebleed, indicating that he needed to finish it before he got back in the pool. He sat down in a lounge chair beside Ant Bite. Ant Bite had a beach towel wrapped around himself and was reading the girl spy book they'd found at camp. His bare feet were propped up, bouncing in time to the steel drums that were set up by the pool.

All the boys from Camp Omigoshee were enjoying an all-expenses-paid trip, thanks to some generous donors and fund-raisers, to make up for the fact that their camp had gotten cut short by the hurricane. In Frederick's opinion, a cruise was better than a transformational disciplinary camp any day. Nothing ever went wrong on cruises.

Then the ship's alarm sounded. There were three shattering blasts on the intercom that made Frederick flinch so badly his straw went up his nose.

Everyone around the pool stopped talking. The drummers quit playing. They looked around, trying to figure out what was happening.

Then Frederick saw a man in a crisp ship's uniform hurrying between the lounge chairs. The man stopped right at the end of Frederick's chair and grabbed a lifeguard's elbow.

"There's a kid overboard," the man said in a low voice to the lifeguard. "He's off the back." Then they both jogged toward the stern of the ship.

Ant Bite swung his feet to the deck and looked at Frederick. "Do you think . . ."

Frederick scrambled off his lounge chair. Ant Bite dropped the book. Nosebleed and the cannonballers climbed, dripping, out of the pool. They thundered to the back of the ship, scattering shuffleboard players and leaving wet footprints on the deck. When they got to the stern, they grabbed the railing and peered out over the dark blue sea stretching to the horizon.

Behind the ship, bobbing on the waves, was one of the orange-and-white lifeboats that was supposed to be hanging from the side of Deck Three. The boat was loaded with what looked like fifty mangoes and a glistening ice sculpture in the shape of a dolphin. Dashiell Blackwood sat at the helm. A red bandanna was tied around his head, and he was driving the boat toward the horizon.

Frederick stepped between the Professor and Joel and leaned against the railing, holding his daiquiri between his hands and watching the boy he had pretended to be sail away.

"Where's he going?" the Professor said, nodding at the boat.

The boys started calling out guesses, but Frederick didn't join them. To tell the truth, he wasn't that curious about where Dashiell Blackwood wound up.

Nosebleed cupped his hands around his mouth. "Bye, Dash!" he yelled.

Dash didn't look back.

Farther down the railing there was a scuffle, and Raj yelled, "Get off me," and the next thing Frederick knew, Raj's black-framed glasses were flying over the railing and dropping into the sea.

Specs let out a triumphant whoop, and then he turned and ran up the deck, his feet pounding. Raj tore after him, cursing. Joel and the boys from Camp Omigoshee followed, leaving Frederick alone at the railing with a few tourists who were pointing at the escaping boy and muttering in concern.

Sunlight sparkled on the water. Frederick finally turned away and followed the others back toward the pool.

There was no way to sugarcoat it. Life could be pretty hard. A lion might horrifically eat you at any moment, even if you were in North America, where lions were not supposed to be. And hurricanes could come right for you, even if you canceled your vacation just to avoid them. And people had all kinds of problems, and sometimes those problems couldn't be fixed.

When Frederick had gotten back home, he'd found that even after his big adventure, he hadn't transformed into *that* guy, that guy who got laughs in class and walked through the school like he owned the place. He still kind of felt like a flea sometimes. And Devin Goodyear was still a lion. So yes, life could be hard. But Frederick had a theory that if—

"Hey, Frederick!"

Frederick looked up. Ant Bite was ahead of him. He'd stopped and was looking back, waiting. He gestured with a hand, beckoning Frederick. "Are you coming or not?"

"Yeah!" Frederick jogged to catch up.

Anyway . . . Frederick had a theory that no matter how hard life was among all the hungry animals, if you could find some people who would help you survive and who you could help in return, and if you took some time off every now and then to get away from your problems, then it could actually be pretty great. And hey, at least it wasn't boring.

Frederick fell into step beside Ant Bite. He plucked the plastic saber out of his drink and dragged a frosty cherry off it with his teeth.

Author's Note

In case you were curious, the book the Professor reads at breakfast is *Lord of the Flies* by William Golding. The spy book Ant Bite has at the end is *I'd Tell You I Love You, but Then I'd Have to Kill You* by Ally Carter.

xoxo Kate

**A hilarious, heartfelt story
about becoming the best fifth grader
in the universe**

Keep reading for a sneak peek!

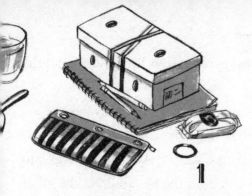

1

A Monstrosity of Science

THE BULLFROG WAS ONLY HALF DEAD, WHICH WAS PERFECT.

He hunkered in the dark culvert under the driveway and gazed at Gertie Reece Foy with a tragical gleam in his eye, as if he knew that her face was the last lovely thing he would ever see.

Gertie stuck her head and shoulders in the culvert and grabbed the frog. His fat legs dangled over her fingers.

She ran to the house and pushed the kitchen door open with her back. Laying the frog on the counter, she ripped open the drawer that held all the unusual and exciting kitchen equipment. She rummaged through cheese graters, bottle openers, and tongs, glancing up every other second to make sure the frog hadn't moved or, worse, *died*.

"What's going on in there?" Aunt Rae yelled from the living room.

"Nothing!" Gertie whipped out the turkey baster.

She wiggled her index finger between the frog's lips—if you could call them lips—and poked the pipette into his mouth. Then she squeezed the blue bulb at the other end, forcing oxygen into his lungs.

The air must have revived him quickly, or maybe he was a little less dead than Gertie had hoped, because he sprang for the edge of the counter. Gertie lunged sideways and cupped her hands over him.

"There, there," she said. "You're safe now."

She peeked at him through her fingers, and he peeked back at her, his eyeballs quivering with gratitude. Or maybe they quivered with rage. It was hard to tell.

She wrapped her hands around the frog's middle, turned on her heel, and crashed into a soft, flowery stomach.

"*Oof,*" said Aunt Rae. She blinked at the frog in Gertie's hands. "What in the Sam Hill are you doing?"

"I resuscitated him." Gertie held the frog closer.

Aunt Rae moved to stand over the air vent in the kitchen floor, and her housedress ballooned around her legs. "You what?"

"Resuscitated," said Gertie. "It means I brought him back to life."

"I *know* what it means." Aunt Rae swayed her weight from foot to foot. *"Why'd* you resuscitate a ugly old bull-frog? That's what I don't know."

Gertie sighed. She spent a lot of time explaining things that should have been obvious to people. "I did it so he could become a miracle of science," she said.

"Huh." Aunt Rae wrinkled her nose at the frog. "Looks more like a monstrosity of science to me."

Gertie gasped. "Oh my Lord."

"What?"

"Aunt Rae, that's even better!"

The monstrosity of science wriggled in her hands, and Gertie tried to hold him tighter but not so much tighter that his eyes would pop right out of his head and fall on the floor.

"I've got to get him in his box, Aunt Rae," Gertie said, "before his eyes roll around on the floor and we have to stick them back."

"Why would—" Aunt Rae began.

"Oh my Lord! I don't have time to explain every little detail!"

"All right, all right." Aunt Rae patted down her skirt.

"But I want you to use bleach on my counter when you're done, you hear me?"

Gertie put the frog and some nice wet leaves in a shoe box. Then she rubber-banded on the lid and went out to the porch. The Zapper-2000, a bug zapper big enough to fry baby dragons, hung from the rafters.

Phase One of the mission was off to a good start.

Gertie always had at least one mission in the works, and she never, *ever* failed to complete her missions. It didn't matter that she wasn't the fastest or the smartest or the tallest, because what made Gertie a force to be reckoned with was the fact that she never gave up. Not ever. Her father liked to say that she was a bulldog with its jaws locked on a car tire.

Gertie was thinking about having that printed on business cards she could hand out to people.

She crouched in the fluorescent blue beam of light beneath the Zapper-2000 and collected a handful of the mosquito bodies that littered the ground. As she worked, the cicadas and crickets started sawing their night song. Gertie stood and watched the sun set on the last day of summer vacation.

With these tasty mosquitoes, the bullfrog was sure to be fat and croaky tomorrow. And with a fat and croaky bullfrog to take with her, Gertie was sure to have the best summer speech of any student at Carroll Elementary. She curled her toes over the edge of the porch boards.

She, Gertie Reece Foy, was going to be the greatest fifth grader in the whole school, world, and universe!

And that was just Phase One.